By the same author

The Falcon's Malteser
Enter Frederick K Bower
The Devil's Door-Bell
The Night of the Scorpion
The Silver Citadel

ANTHONY HOROWITZ

Public Enemy No 2

DRAGON

Dragon
An imprint of the Children's
Division of the Collins Publishing Group
8 Grafton Street, London W1X 3LA

First published in hardback by Collins 1987
Published by Dragon Books 1987

Horowitz, Anthony
Public enemy no. 2.
I. Title
823'.914 [J] PZ7

ISBN 0-583-30888-0

Printed and bound in Great Britain by
Collins, Glasgow

Set in Times

Contents

1
French Dictation

I didn't like Noel Harvey St John Palis from the start. It's a strange thing about French teachers. From my experience they all have either dandruff, bad breath or silly names. Well, Mr Palis had all three, and when you add to that the fact that he was only five foot six with a pot belly, a hearing aid and hair on his neck, you'll agree that he'd never win a Mr Universe contest . . . or a *Combat Monsieur Univers* as he might say.

He'd only been teaching at the school for three months – if you can call his own brand of bullying and sarcasm teaching. Personally I've learnt more from a stick of French bread. I remember the first day he strutted into the classroom. He never walked. He moved his legs like he'd forgotten they were attached to his waist. His feet came first with the rest of his body trying to catch up. Anyway, he wrote his name on the blackboard – just the last bit.

'My name is Palis,' he said.'Pronounced. Pallee. P-A-L-I-S.'

We all knew at once that we'd got a bad one. He hadn't been in the place thirty seconds and already he'd written his name, pronounced it and spelt it out. The next thing he'd be having it embroidered on our uniforms. From that moment on, things got steadily worse. He'd treat the smallest mistake like a personal insult. If you spelt something wrong, he'd make you write it out fifty times. If you mispronounced a word, he'd say you were torturing the language. Then he'd torture you. Twisted ears were his speciality. What can I say? French genders were a nightmare. French tenses have never been more tense. After a few months of Mr Palis, I couldn't even look at a French window without breaking into tears.

Things came to a head as far as I was concerned one Tuesday afternoon in the summer term. We were being given dictation and I leant over and whispered something to a friend. It wasn't anything very witty. I just wanted to know if to give a French dictation you really had to be a French dictator. The trouble was, the friend laughed. Worse still, Mr Palis heard him. His head snapped round so fast his hearing-aid nearly fell off. And somehow his eyes fell on me.

'Yes, Simple?' he said.

'I'm sorry, sir?' I asked with an innocent smile.

'Is there something I should know about? Something to give us all a good laugh?' By now he had strutted forward and my left ear was firmly wedged between his thumb and finger. 'And what is the French for "to laugh", Simple?'

'I don't know, sir,' I winced.

'It is "*rire*". An irregular verb. *Je ris, tu ris, il rit* . . . I think you had better stay behind after school, Simple. And since you seem to like to laugh so much, you can write out for me the infinitive, paticiples, present indicative, past historic, future and present subjunctive tenses of "*rire*". Is that understood?'

'But sir . . .'

'Are you arguing, Simple?'

'No, sir.'

Nobody argued with Mr Palis. Not unless you wanted to spend the rest of the day writing out the infinitive, participles and all the restiples of the French verb *argumenter*.

So that was how I found myself on a sunny afternoon sitting in an empty classroom in an empty school struggling with the complexities of the last verb I felt like using. There was a clock ticking above the door. By four fifteen I'd only got as far as the future. It looked as if my own future wasn't going to be that great. Then the door opened and Boyle and Snape walked in.

They were the last two people I'd expected to see. They were the last two people I wanted to see. Chief Inspector Snape of Scotland Yard and his very un-lovely assistant Boyle. Snape was a great lump of a man who always looked like he was going to burst out of his clothes like the Incredible Hulk. He had pink skin and narrow eyes. Put a pig in a suit and you wouldn't be able to tell the difference until one of them went oink. Boyle was just like I remembered him: black hair – permed on his head, growing wild on his chest. Built like a boxer and I'm not sure if I mean the fighter or the dog. Boyle loved violence. And he hated me. I was only thirteen years old and he seemed to have made it his ambition to make sure that I wouldn't reach fourteen.

'Well, well, well,' Snape muttered. 'It seems we meet again.'

'Pinch me,' I said. 'I must be dreaming.'

Boyle's eyes lit up. 'I'll pinch you!' He started towards me.

'Not now, Boyle!' Snape snapped.

'But he said . . .'

'It was a figure of speech.'

Boyle scratched his head as he tried to figure it out. Snape sat on a desk and picked up an exercise book. 'What's this?' he asked.

'It's French,' I said.

'Yeah? Well it's all Greek to me.' He threw it aside and lit a cigarette. 'So how are you keeping?' he asked.

'What are you doing here?' I replied. I had a feeling they hadn't come to enquire about my health. The only enquiries those two ever made were the sort people were helping them with.

'We came to see you,' Snape said.

'OK. Well, you've seen me now. So if you don't mind . . .' I reached for my satchel.

'Not so fast, laddy. Not so fast.' Snape flicked ash into an ink-well. 'The fact is, Boyle and me, we were wondering . . . we need your help.'

'My help?'

Snape bit his lip. I could see he didn't like asking me. And I could understand it. I was just a kid and he was a big shot in Scotland Yard. It hurt his professional pride. Boyle leant against the wall and scowled. He would rather be hurting me.

'Have you heard of Johnny Powers?' Snape asked.

I shook my head. 'Should I have?'

'He was in the papers last April. The front page. He'd just been sent to jail. He got fifteen years.'

'That's too bad.'

'Sure, Especially as he was only fifteen years old.' Snape blew out smoke. 'The press called him Public Enemy Number One – and for once they were right. Johnny Powers started young . . .'

'How young?'

'He burnt down his kindergarten. He committed his first armed robbery when he was eight years old. Got away with four crates of Mars bars and a ton of sherbet. By the time he was thirteen he was the leader of one of the most dangerous gangs in London. They were called the Catapult Kids . . . which was quite a joke as they were using sawn-off shotguns. Johnny Powers was so crooked he even stole the saw.'

There was a long silence.

'What's this got to do with me?' I asked. Actually, I didn't want to know. But I hate long silences.

'We got Powers last year,' Snape went on. 'Caught him red-handed trying to steal a million pounds of mink from Harrods Department Store. When Johnny went shop-lifting, you were lucky if you were left with the shop.'

'So you've got him,' I said. 'What else do you want?'

'We want the man he was going to sell the furs to.' Snape plunged his cigarette into the ink-well. There was a dull hiss . . . but that might have been Boyle. 'The fence,' he went on. 'The man who buys and distributes all the stolen property in England . . . and in most of Europe too.

'You see, Nick, crime is big business. Robberies, burglaries, hijacks, heists . . . every year a mountain of stuff goes missing. Mink coats. Silver candlesticks. Scotch whisky. Japanese hi-fi. You name it, somebody's stolen it. And recently we've become aware that one man has set up an operation, a fantastic network to handle it – buying and selling.'

'You mean . . . like a shopkeeper?'

'That's just it. He could be a shopkeeper. He could be a banker. He could be anyone. He doesn't get his hands dirty himself, but he's got links with every gang this side of the Iron Curtain. If we could get our hands on him, it would be a disaster for the underworld. And think of what he could tell us! But he's an invisible man. We don't know what he looks like. We don't know where he lives. To us he's just "The Fence". And we want him.'

'We want him,' Boyle repeated.

'I think I get the general idea, Boyle,' I said. I turned back to Snape. 'So why don't you ask this Johnny Powers?' I asked.

Snape lit another cigarette. 'We have asked him,' he replied. 'We offered to half his sentence in return for a name. But Powers is crazy. He refused.'

'Honour amongst thieves,' I muttered.

'Forget that,' Snape said. 'Powers would sell his own grandmother if it suited him. In fact he did sell her. She's now working in an Arabian salt-mine. But he wouldn't sell her to a policeman. He hates policemen. He wouldn't tell us anything. On the other hand, he might just slip the name to someone he knew. Someone he was friendly with . . .'

'What are you getting at?' I asked. I was beginning to feel uneasy. I'd felt uneasy the moment they walked in. But now things were beginning to add up. And it looked like I was the sum total.

'Johnny Powers is fifteen,' Snape went on. 'Too young for prison – but too dangerous for Borstal. So he was sent to a special maximum security centre just outside London – Strangeday Hall. It's for young offenders. No one there is over eighteen. But they're all hardened criminals. We want you to go there.'

'Wait a minute . . . !' I swallowed. 'I'm not a criminal. I'm not even hardened. I'm a softy. I like cuddly toys and the Beano. I'm . . .'

'We'll give you a new name,' Snape cut in. 'A new identity. You'll share a cell with Powers. And as soon as you've found out what we want to know, we'll have you out of there. You'll be back at school before you even know it.'

Out of one prison into another, I thought. But even if I could have skipped the whole term, I wouldn't have considered the offer. Snape might call Powers crazy, but that was the craziest thing I'd ever heard.

'Let me get this straight,' I said. 'You want to lock me up with some under-aged Al Capone in a maximum security jail somewhere outside London. I'm to get friendly with him – preferably before I get my throat cut. And I'm to find out who this fence of yours is so you can arrest him too.'

'That's right.' Snape smiled. 'So what do you say?'

'Forget it! Absolutely not! You must be out of your mind, Snape! Not for a million pounds!'

'Can I take that as a no?' Snape asked.

I grabbed my satchel and stood up. Mr Palis and

his irregular verbs could wait. I just wanted to get out of there. But at the same time, Boyle lurched forward, blocking the way to the door. The look on his face could have blocked a drain.

'Let me persuade him, chief,' he said.

'No, Boyle . . .'

'But . . .'

'He's decided.'

Snape swung himself off the desk. Boyle looked like he was going to explode, but he didn't try to stop me as I reached for the door handle.

'Give me a call if you change your mind,' Snape muttered.

'Don't wait up for it,' I said.

I left the two of them there and walked home. I didn't think I'd hear from them again. I mean, I'd told them what I thought of their crazy idea – and they could always find some other kid. The way I figured it was, they'd just forget about me and go and look for somebody else.

Which just shows you how much I knew.

2
The Purple Peacock

By now you'll be wondering what a nice boy like me could be doing mixed up with two unpleasant types like Snape and Boyle. The answer is a long story. In fact it's a 152-page-long story. I wrote it all down in a book called '*The Falcon's Malteser*'.

It all started with my big brother Herbert. Only that's not what he calls himself. He always wanted to be a private detective and after my parents suddenly decided to emigrate to Australia, he set himself up with an office in Fulham, West London. He called himself Tim Diamond because he thought it would be better for business, and that's what it said on the door: Tim Diamond Inc., Private Detective. The only trouble was, he wasn't too bright. That's putting it mildly. You know the old saying – 'thick as two short planks'? Well, with Herbert you could have built a barn.

Somehow the two of us got mixed up with a Bolivian dwarf, two German killers, a pet alligator and a box of Maltesers that turned out to be worth three and a half million pounds. That was when I met Snape and Boyle. I had more fun meeting the alligator.

But that had been six months ago and right now Herbert and I didn't have two pennies to rub together. If I'd had two pennies he'd have spent them before I had time to rub them together. We'd got a bit of money out of the Maltesers affair but we'd spent most of it on a skiing holiday and medical bills for Herbert's broken leg. We'd have gone National Health, but it was somebody else's leg he broke. The rest had gone on new carpets, new furniture and double glazing for the flat. And now, as they say, we were flat broke.

It was tea-time when I got back. Tea that day was going to be beans on toast. We'd had beans on toast on Saturday and Sunday too. On Monday I'd complained so Herbert had served toast on beans . . . just for a change. There were still sixteen cans of beans left in the larder. What worried me was what we were going to do when we ran out of toast, although the way the bread was looking – curling at the edges and slightly green – it was more likely the toast would run out on us.

There were two letters waiting for me in the hall. One was a card from the local library – an overdue book. It was three months overdue and now it would cost me more to pay the fine than it would have to buy it in the first place. The book was called '*How to make money in your spare time*'. Obviously it hadn't worked. The second letter was post-marked Australia. I could hear Herbert whistling in the kitchen. He was about as musical as the kettle. For some reason I didn't feel like seeing him. I took the letter up to my bedroom, threw my satchel on to the floor and myself on to the bed. Then I read it.

Dearest Nicky (it began),

Just a quick note as Daddy and me are off to another barbecue. It's being given by someone who works with

Daddy, selling doors. We've just had three more doors fitted in my bedroom which is a bit peculiar as they don't lead anywhere. But you know your father. He adores doors.

I hope you are well. I miss you very much and wish you were here with us. I'm sure you'd like Australia. The sun shines all the time (except at night) and there are lots of friendly people. Are you remembering to change your underpants once a week? I am sending you three pairs of Australian underpants in the next post. Just be sure you don't put them on upside-down!

I wish I could come and visit you and Herbert, but I'm very busy with the new baby. We've decided to call her Dora.

Keep well,
Love, Mumsy.

It made me sad, reading the letter. She'd just adopted a new baby – a sister I'd never seen. She didn't care about me any more. She had a new life. Worse still, she hadn't sent me any money. Three pairs of underpants! Maybe I'd be able to trade them in for another tin of beans.

I felt sorry for Dora. If she could have seen what lay ahead of her, she'd have probably toddled back to the orphanage. It's not that there was anything wrong with my parents. But you know how it is. Brush your hair. Clean your teeth. Don't slouch. Don't talk with your mouth full. There were more rules and regulations in my life than the Highway Code and I couldn't even cough without reference to Paragraph 3, Sub-section 5 of the Bringing up Children Act. When my parents emigrated to Australia, I slipped away to live with Herbert. It wasn't much of a choice.

I slipped the letter into a drawer and went back downstairs. By now there was a strange smell in the flat. Any smell that wasn't baked beans would have been strange – and my mouth was watering before I even knew what it was. I stopped on the stairs and sniffed. Fried onions? I hurried into the kitchen.

Herbert was standing by the cooker wearing a pink apron, stirring something in a pan. I glanced at the table. There were two bulging supermarket bags spilling out the sort of stuff I'd have dreamt about if I hadn't been too hungry to sleep. Biscuits, cakes, sausages, eggs, apples and oranges . . .

'What's happened?' I asked. 'No . . . let me guess. You won a raffle? The Salvation Army called? You got a government grant?' I snatched up an apple. 'It's a miracle.'

'No it isn't,' Herbert said indignantly. 'I got a job.'

'That *is* a miracle. You mean . . . somebody paid you?'

'As of today I'm officially employed – in pursuit of the purple peacock.' Herbert turned back to the frying pan. 'How do you want your steak?' he asked. 'Rare, medium or well done?'

'Large,' I said.

Ten minutes later we sat down and ate the equivalent of a week's suppers rolled into one. There are times when I'm genuinely fond of my big, blue-eyed brother. All right, so he couldn't solve a crossword let alone a crime. He had trouble tying his own shoe-laces and he was afraid of the dark. But we'd lived together for three years now and things could have been a lot worse. They were about to get a lot worse as a matter of fact – but of course I didn't know that then.

'What's the news from Australia?' he asked over the chocolate mousse.

'Nothing much,' I said.

'Did Mum send you any money?'

'No. But she's going to send me some underpants.'

'Underpants!' Herbert shook his head. 'That's an affront.'

'Actually it's a Y-front.' I finished my pudding and threw down the spoon. 'All right, Tim,' I said. 'What's all this about the purple peacock?'

'I've got to find it,' Herbert explained. 'It's gone missing.'

'From a zoo?'

'From a museum.' Herbert smiled. 'It's not an animal. It's a vase.'

He pushed the plates to one side and took out a notebook. His eyes had narrowed and his mouth was stretched tightly. This was the way he looked when he was trying to be a private detective. I don't know who he thought he was kidding. Not this kid anyway.

'It's a Ming vase,' he went on. 'Nine inches high, blue and white with a purple peacock enamelled on the side.' He flipped the notebook open. 'It's fifteenth century. Made for the Emperor Chēng-Hua.'

'Chēng who?' I asked.

'No. Chēng-Hua. A Chinese orange.' He looked at the notebook again. 'I mean, a Chinese mandarin. Anyway, he was a big-wig. And he had this vase made.'

'Is it valuable?'

'Valuable?' He leant back in his chair, spilling wine down his shirt. 'It's worth a mint – and I'm not talking Polos. There's only one vase like it in the world. It's worth thousands. For the last seventy years it's been on display in the British Museum. Then, a week ago, they sent it to be cleaned. Only it never got there. It went into the van at 9.35 A.M. exactly.'

'And when the van arrived . . .'

'The van never arrived. It vanished too. The driver stopped at a garage in Camden. He went in to pay for the petrol. When he got back to the pump, the van was gone.'

'With the vase inside.'

'That's right.'

'So why hasn't the museum gone to the police?' I asked. 'Why come to you?'

'They're too embarrassed to go to the police, Nick. I mean, that Ming was priceless. The museum wants it. But they don't want a scandal.' He gave me a lop-sided smile. 'This is a case for Tim Diamond.'

A nut-case, I thought. But I said, 'How did they find you?'

'Well . . . er . . .' Herbert hesitated. I could see he wished I hadn't asked him that. 'As a matter of fact, Aunty Maureen recommended me.'

'Aunty Maureen of Slough with the false hip?'

'Yes.' He was almost grumpy now. I doubt if Sherlock Holmes or Mike Hammer ever got recommended for a case by their aunties. 'She knows one of the guards. Anyway . . .' He sniffed. '. . .

I'm the right man for the job. If they want to find their priceless vase I'll crack it.'

'You probably will,' I said.

Herbert poured himself some more wine. I looked down at the table. Perhaps I was being a bit hard on him. After all, he'd just paid for the best meal we'd had in weeks. That reminded me of the most important issue at hand.

'How much did they pay you?' I asked.

The smile returned to his face. 'A hundred in advance,' he said. 'Plus ten pounds a day in expenses.'

'Ten pounds!'

'Well . . .' Herbert shrugged. 'I have expensive expenses.'

'That's great.' Even as I said it, my mind was ticking over. But I wasn't thinking about vases.

There was about to be a school trip to Woburn Abbey; the stately home and wildlife park. Now I'm not exactly into stately homes – old suits of armour and dry, dusty paintings by dry, dusty painters – but the park sounded fun, hurling stale doughnuts at the lions and getting a few laughs from the giraffes. The only problem was, we were expected to contribute to the cost: three pounds a head. I'd already missed out on Hampton Court and the Greenwich observatory and the class was beginning to look on me as a charity case. They'd even had a whip-round for me. Not that I needed a whip, but it's the thought that counts.

All week I'd been wondering how to get a loan out of Herbert but I hadn't had the heart to ask. It would only have reminded him of his own situation and I hate to see a grown man cry. But one hundred pounds in advance and ten pounds a day in expenses . . . ?

'Tim . . .' I muttered.

'Yes?'

'Since you've got a bit of cash now, do you think you could lend me a fiver?'

'A fiver?'

'You know . . . for Woburn Abbey.'

He considered for a moment. 'But that's a whole half-day's expenses,' he complained.

'Well, you could always stay in bed until lunchtime.' He was unconvinced so I had one last try. 'It's part of my education,' I went on. 'What would Mum and Dad say? We're talking about my whole future . . .'

He didn't like it, but he couldn't argue. He sighed and dug into his pocket. 'All right,' he sighed. 'But you do the washing up.'

He threw a crumpled five pound note on to the table. I snatched it up. It had been so long since I'd seen a five pound note, I'd even forgotten what colour it was.

'Thanks a bunch,' I said, wishing he had given me a whole bunch. I tucked the fiver into my shirt pocket. 'So when do you start looking for the purple peacock?' I asked.

'Tomorrow.' Herbert lifted his wine-glass. 'I reckon I'll go back to the garage in Camden. Find the pump assistant.'

'And then?'

'I'll pump her.'

He threw back the wine in one. I think it was

meant to be a dramatic gesture, but it must have gone the wrong way because his face went bright red and a second later he made a dramatic dash for the loo.

I watched him go. In all the excitement I'd forgotten to tell him about Snape and Boyle. But in truth I'd more or less forgotten about them myself.

3
Woburn Abbey

So that was how I found myself, a few days later, beetling up the M1 at fifty miles an hour on the way to Woburn Abbey. There were forty of us in the coach – thirty-eight pupils and two teachers. My friend Monsieur Palis was one of them. The other was an old guy by the name of Snelgrove. He had been teaching history for so long that I reckon he must have been alive when most of it was going on.

We'd all been given packed lunches which we'd unpacked and eaten before we'd even hit the motorway. Now the coach was strewn with crisp packets, sweet wrappers and crusts of Mother's Pride. The driver couldn't have looked much happier if he'd been driving a hearse. I'd managed to grab a place in the back row and we were all making faces at the other motorists to see who could be the first to cause a multiple pile-up. Woburn Abbey was about an hour from London. Snelgrove had spent the first fifteen minutes giving us a potted history of the place, which Palis had then translated into French. Nobody had listened. The sun was shining. If we'd wanted a history lesson, we'd have stayed at school.

At last we turned off the M1 and after rattling down a few country lanes and doubtless flattening a few country hedgehogs, we reached the grounds of the abbey itself. There was a sign pointing one way to the stately home and another to the safari park.

Naturally we followed the first. I shifted on my seat and felt something jutting into my leg. Somebody had left a catapult – a cheap, plastic thing – wedged in the side of the chair. Without really thinking I pocketed it. And that was all I had on me when we finally arrived: that and a couple of pounds in change from Herbert's fiver.

The coach reached the car-park and rumbled to a halt. We were all about to rush for the door, but then Palis stood up, raising a hand.

'Gentlemen . . .' he began.

I looked around me. I could see thirty-eight hooligans, but certainly no gentlemen.

'. . . may I remind you,' he went on, 'that this is an historic outing. Woburn Abbey is a stately home, not an amusement arcade. In fact the Marquess and Marchioness of Tavistock are still in residence here. So if there is any misbehaviour, any tomfoolery, I shall deal with the matter personally.'

His hand lashed out, sending a boy called Sington in a backward somersault down the aisle.

'And no chewing gum during the tour,' Palis added with a twitch of a smile.

We trooped out more sheepishly after that. Even old Snelgrove seemed afraid of Palis. Two by two we marched down a winding path, past the restaurant and through the turnstile. There was a sign up beside the ticket booth.

SPECIAL EXHIBITION
The Woburn Carbuncles
On display in the State Salon

'Please sir,' somebody asked. 'What's a carbuncle?'

'It's a type of jewel,' Snelgrove whispered, glancing nervously at Palis. 'Quite a large jewel. It's normally red and . . .'

'No talking!' Palis snapped.

Snelgrove whimpered. Sington gave a strangled cough as he tried to dislodge the chewing-gum from the back of his throat. Palis strutted forward.

We really were having a lot of fun.

We went through a small door set in the side of the house. The tradesman's entrance with a capital T – except that here it stood for tourists. This was the summer season and the place was packed: Americans, Germans, Japanese . . . enough nationalities to start a world war. The entrance led you straight into the gift-shop which was a pretty neat coincidence. There were all sorts of traditional and historic items on sale such as tea-towels, furry hot-water bottles and royal mugs. There were even a few mugs buying them. I stopped to flick through the postcards, thinking I might get one for Herbert. It was the sort of gesture he'd appreciate and they were only 8p. But then Palis called out 'This way!' and we all hurried off to the left.

I'm probably not the best person to describe a stately home. See one and you've seen them all as far as I'm concerned, and I wouldn't exactly get into a state if I didn't see any. I mean, tapestries and paintings and chandeliers and fancy tables are fine if you like that sort of thing in your front room. But just following a red rope around the place gawping at them . . . well, it's not my cup of tea – even if the cup is three hundred years old and was once used by the Earl of Southampton.

So I was bored by the book room, sent to sleep by the staircase and I was hardly drawn to the drawing room either. You wouldn't believe how much stuff there was in that place. Paintings, mirrors, bronze clocks – you name it, at some time or other they'd bought it. By the time we got to Queen Victoria's bedroom, I'd have gladly thrown myself into the bed, even if the old girl had been in it at the time.

The worst of it was, of course, that Palis and Snelgrove were lapping it all up. They lingered in every room and while Snelgrove droned on about one thing, Palis would be pointing our attention to another. I was surprised he knew so much about it. After all, it wasn't as if any of it was French.

And what I didn't know was that every step I took, every minute that dragged past was carrying me closer to a horrible nightmare. Palis was wrong. Compared with what was about to happen, Woburn Abbey really was a funfair.

Our progress through the house had been watched by a number of antique ladies sitting in equally antique chairs. They were the only security on view and they looked about as lethal as a box of After Eights. Half of them were knitting. The other half were smiling sweetly and blinking behind their horn-rimmed spectacles. But as we shuffled towards the Grand Salon, I noticed two security guards in uniform standing beside the door. One of them brushed against me as I went through. He didn't apologize.

The Grand Salon was like any other room in the

house. Which is to say, it was certainly grand. This one was furnished in blue with blue chairs and sofas and blue murals on the walls. But the reason for the security guards wasn't blue at all. It was bright red. There were a dozen of them, glittering in a case in the centre of the room. The Woburn Carbuncles – very pretty and doubtless worth a pretty penny.

'Apparently the Marquess of Tavistock discovered them in the attic,' I heard Snelgrove say.

Lucky Marquess, I thought to myself. All we'd ever found in our attic was dry rot.

'Aren't they beautiful, boys?' Snelgrove went on.

'This way!' Palis cried and went on himself.

We followed.

I was the last to leave the room. For some reason there were no tourists behind me. Even then I thought it was strange. There had been at least twenty other people in every room we'd visited but suddenly there was no one at all. I walked towards the door. At the same moment, there was a crash of breaking glass. A bell went off. I turned and looked back.

It was impossible. A minute ago I'd been looking at a glass-topped cabinet with twelve red carbuncles inside. Now I was looking at a shattered cabinet with only eleven carbuncles lying in the wreckage. But apart from the security guards, there was nobody in the room. Someone had just stolen part of the Woburn windfall. The alarm bell was still ringing. But I knew it wasn't me and it couldn't have been them so . . .

'All right, sonny. Stay where you are . . .'

The two guards were walking towards me, the

splinters of glass crunching on the carpet beneath their feet. I looked over my shoulder. All the kids from the school were jammed into the doorway, staring at me.

'What's going on?' Palis called out from behind them. A moment later he had pushed his way through and was standing there breathing down my neck. With his breath, he was probably staining my collar.

'Give it back, son,' the security guard muttered, holding out one hand. He was moving very slowly, like I was dangerous or something. 'You can't get away with it.'

'Get away with what?' I squeaked. My voice seemed to have climbed up my nose and hidden behind my eyes.

Palis gazed at the ruined cabinet. 'Simple . . .' he quivered.

'I haven't . . .' I began.

As I spoke, I pushed my hands into my pockets. I wanted to show them that they were empty, that it was all a terrible mistake. But before I could say another word, my palm came into contact with something cold and round. I took it out. It glittered in the sunlight.

'Simple!' Palis hissed the S out like a snake.

'Wait a minute . . .' I said.

But it was clear that nobody had any intention of waiting a minute. If Palis didn't grab me, the guards would. The bell was still ringing and now I could hear other voices shouting in the corridor. Perhaps half a second passed – enough time for an instant playback and an even more instant decision. It was a frame-up. It had to be. Somebody had slipped the jewel into my pocket. Who? I remembered the guard jostling me as I went into the Grand Salon, the same guard who was now about six feet away from me and getting closer. It didn't make sense. But it had to be him. He'd been in the room. He'd seen . . .

An instant decision. I stuffed the jewel back in my pocket, turned and ran.

The guard shouted something after me. Palis reached out. Somehow I twisted out of his grip and then I was pushing my way through my own friends, hoping that none of them would try to stop me. At least I was right about that. They did quite the opposite, crowding around the door and stopping Palis and the two guards who were already trying to force their way after me.

I paused for breath beside a window. At the same moment, there was a sudden wailing and six police cars, blue lights flashing, tore up the drive and screeched to a halt outside. It was impossible. They couldn't possibly have got there that fast. My stomach shrank like a punctured football. It was a frame-up all right. But it didn't just stop with the two security guards. It had been organized on a massive scale.

About twenty-four policemen were scattering across the drive, moving to surround the house. Palis had almost broken through the barrier of schoolboys. This was no time to ask questions. It was crazy of course. Even if I could get out of the house, I had nowhere to go. But right then I didn't care. I just wanted to get out. I could ask questions later.

I looked round. I was in the State Dining Room. A dozen dukes and duchesses stared down at me accusingly from the walls. In the middle of the room there was a table set for eight – eight guests who would never arrive. Perfect white porcelain, gleaming silver cutlery and slender glasses stood on the polished surface to be admired by the passing tourists. There was a door at the other end of the room. I made for it.

But I hadn't taken two steps before my way was blocked. One of the antique ladies, roused by the bell and the shouting, stood there, holding a half-finished pink cardigan on two knitting needles. She was about sixty, dressed in a two-piece suit with permed hair and two angry red spots in her cheeks.

'Stop him!' Palis yelled out behind me.

The old lady's lips pouted in anger. She must have thought I was a vandal or something. 'Oh you beast!' she exclaimed. 'You little beast!'

She jerked her hands. The pink cardigan fell to the ground and suddenly she was holding the two knitting needles above her head as if they were daggers, the points pointing at me.

'You beast!' she shrilled for a third time and, with her eyes blazing, charged towards me. At the same time, I ran towards her.

About one second later we met.

I didn't mean to do it. I don't know what I meant to do. But she could have killed me with those needles and I had to defend myself. As she stabbed downwards, I ducked. My shoulder went into her stomach in a sort of insane rugby tackle. I heaved upwards. And then she was soaring through the air, carried by her own momentum, a whirling mass of tweed suit, nylon stocking and stainless steel knitting needle. With a little screech she landed on the dinner table then slid all the way down with an explosion of shattering plates and glasses and clattering knives and forks. The polished wood offered no resistance. She shot off the other end like a rocket, hit the wall and finally disappeared as, with a resounding crash, one of the portraits fell on top of her. I didn't see what state she was in after that. I was already gone.

I found myself in yet another, smaller room: some sort of library. A third guard was struggling out of his chair as I approached. I pushed him back with the flat of my hand and sighed as he crashed into a shelf, instantly disappearing in an avalanche of books. There was a long corridor leading off to the left, but even as I considered it, a policeman appeared at the far end and began to run towards me. I continued straight ahead, through an alcove and into a second, huge drawing room. A red rope hung across the entrance. I jumped over it and ran on.

I looked back to see if anyone was following. Somehow my elbow caught one of the marble busts, knocking it off the shelf. It bust. But at least there was no one in sight. In fact I seemed to have left the bell, the tourists and the police behind me. Things were quieter here. I turned a corner and found myself face to face with a guard dog. A

Pekinese. It must have been all of six inches high. I smiled. It bit me in the ankle. I kicked it. It fled.

I realized now that I had found my way into the private parts of Woburn Abbey, the parts that other peers can't reach. In many ways it was just as grand as the public part. But it was also more real. There were things like newspapers and cheap paperbacks scattered amongst the antiques. Someone had perched a hat on top of one of the statues. A pair of slippers lay beside a chair.

'Try that way . . . !'

The voice reached me from the distance. I hurried on. I might be in the private parts, but if I didn't move quickly, someone would soon be grabbing me by mine.

I ducked down a corridor, searching for a way out. I heard a door open and footsteps on wood. Somebody was heading towards me. I reached out for the first door I came to, opened it and slipped inside.

'What are you doing?'

I spun round. I was in a bathroom – all white marble and shining brass taps. And I wasn't alone. There was a large, pink-faced man in the bath, up to his neck in bubbles, reading a copy of '*Country Life*'. He was staring at me through big square glasses that had all steamed up.

'Who are you?' I asked. I couldn't think of anything to say.

'I am the Marquess.'

'The Marquess of Bath?'

'No. The Marquess of Tavistock.' He frowned. 'But I'm in the bath.'

I smiled at him.

'Get out!' he demanded.

I got out.

There was an open window at the end of the corridor. It led on to a narrow balcony running along the side of the house. My luck was still holding out. There was nobody in sight. Quickly, I hoisted myself over the edge, clinging on with both hands. For a moment I hung there. Then I dropped. It was a long way. A bank of grass broke my fall. It also broke my leg – at least, that's what it felt like. But when I got up I found I could just about stand. I'd twisted my ankle and torn my trousers. But at least I was out.

I limped round the back of the house and through a wrought-iron gate. From here the path led me back to the door where the tour had begun. There were about a hundred people milling around outside – mainly tourists but also a few policemen. As three more of them raced into the house, I hurried forward as fast as I could, looking for shelter in the crowd. Once again luck was on my side. It seemed that although the police knew there was a thief in Woburn Abbey, they didn't yet know that the thief was thirteen years old. Two more policemen ran past me as I made my way back to the turnstile. They didn't try to stop me.

I had got as far as the car-park before I realized that I had no idea where I was going. After all, I couldn't just get into the coach and expect them to take me back to school. And running was out of the question. Quite apart from my ankle, the fields around Woburn Abbey were flat and wide. I'd be spotted a mile away. Worse still, the police were streaming out of the building now. They must have discovered my escape route. Which meant they would know who they were looking for.

And everything I'd done up to now had only made matters worse. Perhaps I could have explained away the jewel in my pocket. Even if they hadn't believed me, I could have put it down to a schoolboy prank. I could have told them I was going to give it to charity. But I'd also hurled an old lady through the air. I'd smashed hundreds of pounds worth of plates and glass. I dare say the Marquess wasn't too pleased with me either. I was up a well-known creek and I still had no idea how I'd got there.

Desperately I looked about me; at the cars parked in neat rows, at the families strolling towards the abbey wondering what all the fuss was about, at the first policemen rapidly approaching. I was thinking on my feet. I could barely stand on my feet. My ankle was doing a good impersonation of a barrage balloon. I had nowhere to go, no way of getting there.

Then I saw the Landrover. It was parked at the end of a row, with no one around. The doors would be locked of course, but there was something on the roof, covered with a sheet of tarpaulin. But the tarpaulin hadn't been tied down properly. There was a gap.

Without a second thought I climbed up the back of the Landrover and crawled through. There were a whole lot of sacks on the roof, filled with some sort of grain. Either the driver was a farmer or a health-food fanatic. There was just enough space for me. I lay there in the darkness, listening to my heart thumping. I'd just made it in time. I heard the crunch of footsteps on gravel.

'You see him?' somebody asked.

'No.'

'Thirteen years old. Scruffy. And dangerous.'

'Try over there . . .'

About two minutes later – it could have been twenty minutes later – there were more footsteps and the sound of a man and a woman talking in low voices. I heard the Landrover doors open and close. There was a rattle as the engine started and the whole vehicle shook. Then I felt myself pressed against the sacks as the Landrover jerked forward. We were away!

Given more time, the police might have set up a road-block and searched every car as it left the abbey. But we weren't stopped as we trundled out, travelling at about ten miles an hour. I couldn't see anything under the tarpaulin and I didn't dare look. I just hoped that wherever the Landrover was heading it was somewhere a long way away – preferably New Zealand. I imagined we'd hit the M1 pretty soon. After that I'd be safe, at least for the time being.

But we didn't go anywhere near the motorway. The driver seemed to be in no hurry. Ten minutes later we were still moving along at a snail's pace. It was getting hot under the tarpaulin with the sun beating down. I could hardly breathe. Carefully I reached out, lifted up the loose flap and looked out.

We were in a traffic jam – just what I needed. There were at least six cars behind us. I couldn't see how many more in front. The road was following a tall silver fence with a second, lower fence behind it. Otherwise all I could see was fields and trees. The Landrover rattled as it passed over a cattle grid. The sacks bounced. So did I. There was some sort of lodge on the other side of the road. Afraid of being seen, I crawled back under the tarpaulin.

Stop and start, stop and start. We didn't seem to be going anywhere and we were taking an awful long time getting there. I peeked out again, just in time to read a notice on a wooden board beside the road. 'Please put your radio aerials down,' it said. Put your aerials down? Where was the road leading? Under a low bridge?

The Landrover stopped again. I didn't dare look out, but I heard voices.

'Have you got any pets in the car?' a woman asked.

'No.' That was the driver.

'Here you are . . .'

'Thank you.'

So we weren't carrying any pets. That was really nice to know. But what had that got to do with anything? Where were we? I was almost suffocating. We were still crawling along and the sun was hotter than ever. Something dripped on to the roof. For a minute I thought I was crying. I wouldn't have been surprised. But it was only sweat. By now I'd decided to clear off at the first opportunity. Getting on to the Landrover had been a mistake in the first place. I'd just have to leg it cross-country.

About another fifteen minutes passed before I'd had enough. We'd stopped and started more times than I could count and I had no idea where I was. But at least I was out of the abbey. Throwing caution to the winds, I shifted on the roof and slithered out from under the tarpaulin. Without looking round, I dropped to the grass. My ankle screamed at me. Ignoring it, I ran. Only when I was twenty yards from the Landrover did I stop and take my bearings.

I was in a field, penned in. A fence ran the whole length, boarded at the top, like something out of Colditz. The Landrover was standing in line with about a dozen cars on either side. A picnic area. That was my first thought. But why should anyone want to have a picnic here? It was a rough, uneven field with knotted grass and bumpy hillocks. A few trees twisted upwards here and there. The road we'd been following zig-zagged all the way from the fence. I looked at the cars. Despite the weather, all the windows were rolled up. The people inside were waving at me and pointing. They didn't look like they were inviting me to a picnic.

Then a loudspeaker crackled into life and a voice floated across the grass. Floated? It flew, carried by its own urgency.

'Get back in the car!' it commanded. 'Get back in the car!'

And at the same time I heard a low, angry growling that sent my heart scuttling into my mouth and made the hairs on the back of my neck stand up like a pin-cushion. I turned round.

A full-sized lion was padding slowly towards me.

I still don't know how I managed to avoid wetting myself. I couldn't believe what I'd just done. I'd sat on top of a Landrover and let it drive me straight into the middle of the safari park. Where else do you go after you've visited Woburn Abbey? And then, when we were nicely settled in the lion compound, I'd got off. Couldn't I at least have waited for the giraffes? Giraffes are vegetarians. The lion obviously wasn't.

It was snarling at me, its mouth open. I could see all the way down the back of its throat. Any minute now I'd be getting an inside view. The lion was huge. You could have made twenty furry hot-water bottles out of its mane alone. But that wasn't what I was looking at. I was looking at its teeth: horrible sharp teeth glistening in the sunlight. And the lion was looking at me. Its ugly brown eyes were burning with anger. And hunger.

It can't be much fun being a lion in a safari park. All day long you sit there watching your lunch drive past in little metal boxes. Canned food. Well, this food had just got out of the can. And the lion was going to make a meal of it in every sense of the word.

There was an orange and black jeep tearing across the grass towards me. But by the time it arrived it would be too late. I wanted to run for it, but there was no chance. The other cars were too far away and my legs had turned to jelly . . . jelly that hadn't even set. The lion growled again, about to leap. I was alone, unarmed.

Unarmed . . .

Suddenly I remembered the catapult that I'd found on the coach. My hand fumbled its way into my pocket and pulled it out. All I needed was a stone, some sort of missile. But there were no stones. Just grass and a few twigs. The lion edged forward. There was nothing in sight. Not even a pebble.

And then I remembered the Woburn carbuncle.

I'd pulled it out before I even realized what I was doing. It glittered, a brilliant red, about the size of a ping-pong ball. The lion's snarl became a roar. My hand was shaking like a leaf but somehow I managed to load the catapult, pulled on the elastic. The lion leapt. I fired.

It was still roaring, its mouth open as the carbuncle flashed through the air. At the same time, I threw myself to one side.

The carbuncle disappeared down the lion's throat.

I rolled over and looked round. The lion had missed me by about a yard. It was lying on its back and for a crazy moment I was reminded of Sington in the coach with the chewing-gum. The carbuncle had lodged itself in the creature's wind-pipe. It was kicking its legs feebly in the air, choking and whimpering like a stray cat. Weakly, I got to my feet.

I just had time to see another three lions come strolling over the hill to find out what was happening when the jeep arrived. A warden was standing up in the passenger seat, aiming a rifle with an anaesthetic dart. He fired and missed. There was a sharp pain in my thigh and the world began to spin.

I blacked out. But before I went, I realized that the warden hadn't missed after all. He'd been aiming at me all the time. He must have decided that I was more dangerous than the lion.

4

Trial and Error

In the end I was accused of theft, assault, trespass, criminal damage and cruelty to animals. The lion survived by the way. It was on the operating table for six hours to remove the carbuncle. The bad news for the surgeon was it woke up after five.

I was sent to the Old Bailey to be tried – number three court. I still remember it. It was far smaller than I'd imagined it would be, walled in with wooden panels but with clear glass windows in the roof. It was like standing in a cross between a chapel and a squash court. The jury sat along one side – twelve men just and true. They may have been true but half the time they were only just awake. And in the middle there was a whole cluster of barristers and court-officials in their black robes and white bows, looking like the sort of gift-wrapped parcels you might take to a funeral.

I was in the dock, of course, with two policemen close behind me. The dock was too high for me so someone had slid an old suitcase there for me to stand on. After I'd been asked a question I did say 'I rest my case' but nobody got the joke. In fact nobody was looking very happy at all. Counsel for the prosecution couldn't even glance at me without grinding his teeth. The judge was too old to have any teeth but looked like he'd have been glad to grind someone else's. As for my counsel for the defence, he kept on sighing and mopping his face with a handkerchief. He knew a hopeless case when he saw one.

The public gallery, high above me, was full. My arrest had been front page news in all the papers and the reporters were there now, scribbling away in notepads and (they weren't allowed cameras) drawing thumb-nail sketches. Not that I knew why anyone would be interested in a reporter's thumbnail. In fact I found the whole thing a bit of a trial. Which is to say it was about as interesting as double algebra on a wet afternoon. These legal people seemed to take an hour to say what you and I could manage in a minute. They couldn't even say 'Good morning' without written evidence from the weather office and three precedents to prove their point.

Things livened up though when the witnesses arrived. First on was the old lady from Woburn Abbey – now in tweed neck-brace and matching splints. She described how I'd attacked her and thrown her along the dinner table only somehow she forgot to mention that she'd been the one with the knitting needles.

'What happened after you hit the table?' counsel for the defence asked.

'An old master fell on me.'

'Are you referring to the Marquess of Tavistock?'

'No.' she sniffed. 'It was a painting.'

That brought a titter of laughter from the public gallery. The judge banged his hammer and not for the first time I was tempted to shout out 'Sold to the lady with the neck-brace and knitting needles.' But I kept my mouth shut.

'No further questions,' defence muttered miserably.

The prosecution called two more security guards and the ranger from the safari park. They all told much the same story. I'd been caught red-handed with the carbuncle. I'd fought my way out. I'd half-killed a lion. I'd finally been arrested. I was just grateful they didn't call the lion.

The last prosecution witness was a complete surprise. Noel Harvey St John Palis took the oath and strutted into the witness box where he stood with his pot belly pressing against the wood. Even more surprising were the things he said about me. I'd figured he'd take the opportunity to add a bit to my sentence. After all, he'd always liked long sentences in dictation. But in fact he described me as hard-working, intelligent and honest. He said he was amazed by my crimes. True, he spoilt it all by adding that there could be no doubt of my guilt. But it's the thought that counts.

Then it was the turn of the defence.

My counsel was a thin, grey-haired man by the name of Garrod. Perry Mason he was not. We'd met before the trial and I'd asked him how he was going to get me off the hook. He'd laughed at that. He didn't laugh often. You almost expected to see cobwebs at the corners of his mouth.

'Get you off?' he asked. 'I can't get you off. The evidence against you is overwhelming. It's rock solid. It's massive!'

'But I was framed.'

'So was the old lady you attacked. A picture fell on her.' He mopped himself with the handkerchief.

‘All I can do is persuade the judge that, at heart, you’re a nice boy,’ he said. He looked at me and wrinkled his nose. ‘Of course, that won’t be easy. But this is a first offence. Perhaps he’ll go easy on you.’

‘How easy?’ I asked.

Garrod shrugged. ’Six months . . . ?’

‘Prison!’ I stared at him. ‘I can’t go to prison! I’m innocent!’

‘Of course.’ He sighed. ‘Until you’re proved guilty.’

So Garrod set out to prove that despite appearances I was a nice guy. To do this he called a succession of character witnesses. Unfortunately for me, he’d chosen the wrong characters. Aunty Maureen was the first – she of Slough and the false hip. I hadn’t seen her for a few years. The way she carried on in court, it looked like it would be quite a few years before I saw her again. She was fine with Garrod. She told him how I’d visited her in hospital and given her flowers and didn’t even mention that I’d pinched them from the next bed. But when she was cross-examined she got . . . well, cross.

‘Don’t you talk to me like that!’ she shrilled at the prosecution counsel. ‘I’m a senior citizen. I got blown up in the last war. I stepped on a bomb.’

‘Mine?’ the prosecution counsel asked.

‘I don’t know whose it was. But I tell you this. My little Nick would never nick nothing . . .’

‘Objection!’ the prosecution counsel cried.

‘Don’t you call me an objection! If you want to call me names you can come and see me later.’

To illustrate the point, she reached down and

heaved. There was a loud click and a moment later she was waving part of her false leg at the judge. I groaned. There was an uproar in the court. The pressmen laughed. Aunty Maureen was dragged out by a policewoman, still struggling and waving her false leg. My defence counsel sat down in a little heap. His professional reputation had just crawled out of the courtroom waving a white flag.

I was beginning to think things couldn't get worse. Then the court usher called out 'Herbert Timothy Simple' and my big brother walked in.

He'd dressed up in a suit for the occasion and I noticed he was wearing a black tie. Had he put it on by accident, I wondered, or did he know something I didn't? He'd only been to see me once since my arrest. The police had told him what had happened and our conversation had gone something like this.

'I don't believe it,' he'd said.

'I didn't do it,' I said.

'I don't believe you,' he'd said.

'You mean you don't believe that I didn't do what you don't believe I did?'

He'd just blinked at that. And chewed his bus-ticket.

And now here he was, still looking dazed. But then he caught my eye and smiled. I could see he was trembling like a leaf. Anyone would think it was him who was on trial.

The court usher handed him a bible. He took it, nodded and tried to put it in his pocket. The court usher snatched it back. I thought there was going to be another fight but then the judge explained that

Herbert was meant to use the bible to take the oath. Herbert blushed.

'Sorry, your highness,' he muttered.

The judge frowned. 'You can address me as your worship.'

'Oh yes . . .' Herbert was going to pieces and he hadn't exactly been together to start with. 'Sorry, your highship.'

The court usher moved forward and tried again. 'I swear to tell the truth,' he said.

'Do you?' Herbert asked.

'No – you do!' The usher closed his eyes.

'Just repeat the words, Mr Simple,' the judge sighed.

At last the oath was taken. Garrod got up and walked over to the witness box, moving like an old man. Herbert smiled at him.

'You are Herbert Timothy Simple?' Garrod asked.

'Am I?' Herbert sounded astonished.

'Are you Herbert Timothy Simple?' the judge demanded.

'Yes . . . yes, of course I am, your parsnip,' Herbert said.

Garrod took a deep breath. 'Could you describe your brother for us?' he asked.

'Well, he's about five foot two, dark hair, quite thin . . .'

Counsel for the defence shuddered and I thought he was going to have some sort of attack. His cheeks were pinched and his wig was crooked. 'We know what he looks like, Mr Simple,' he whimpered. 'We just want to know what sort of person he is.'

Herbert thought for a minute.

'Answer the question,' the judge muttered.

'Certainly, your cowslip,' Herbert said. 'Nick's all right. I mean . . . for a kid brother. The one trouble is, he's really untidy. He's always leaving his books in the kitchen and . . .'

'We are not interested in your kitchen!' Garrod groaned. He was fighting to keep his patience. But it was a losing battle. 'What we want to know is, looking at him now, would you say he had it in him to brutally assault an old lady and steal a priceless jewel?'

Herbert gave me a big smile and nodded. 'Oh yes. Absolutely!'

Garrod was about to ask another question but now he stopped, his mouth wide open. 'You can't say that!' he squeaked. 'He's your brother!'

'But you told me to tell the truth,' Herbert protested. 'The truth, the whole truth and nothing but the truth.'

There was another uproar in the court. The judge banged his hammer. Herbert had cooked my goose all right – feathers and all. After his testimony, the judge would throw the book at me. But that was nothing compared with what I planned to throw at Herbert.

Garrod sank back into his seat. 'No more questions,' he said.

'Does that mean I can leave the witless box?' Herbert asked.

Nobody stopped him. The trial was more or less over.

The jury took forty-five seconds to reach its verdict. Guilty, of course. Then it was the time for the sentence. The policeman made me stand up. The judge glared at me.

'Nicholas David Simple,' he began. 'You have been found guilty on all five charges. It is now my duty to sentence you.

'Your crime was a particularly unpleasant one. You are, if I may say, a particularly unpleasant criminal. You stole a priceless object, part of the national heritage. You viciously assaulted an old lady and a lion. You caused thousands of pounds worth of damage. And for what? Doubtless you would have squandered your profits on pop music, on violent video cassettes, on glue which you would then sniff.'

He sniffed himself. Then he bent his fingers until the bones clicked.

'Society must be protected from the likes of you,' he went on. 'If you were older, the sentence would be more severe. As it is, it is the sentence of this court that you will go to prison for eighteen months.' He banged his hammer. 'Court adjourned.'

Things happened very quickly after that.

The two policemen dragged me out of the courtroom, down a flight of stairs. My hands were cuffed in front of me and I was led down a passage to a door. Outside, in an underground car-park, a van was waiting.

'In you get,' one of the policemen said.

On my way up – before I'd been tried – I'd been 'son' or 'Nick'. Now I didn't have a name. A hand pushed me in the small of my back. And my back had never felt smaller. It was like I'd somehow shrunk.

'But I'm innocent,' I mumbled.

The policemen ignored me.

Two of them got in after me. The doors were locked and the van drove away. There was one small window in the back, heavily barred. The frosted glass broke the whole world up into tear-drops. We reached the surface. The Old Bailey, Holborn . . . London slipped away behind me. The policemen didn't speak. One of them was reading a newspaper. My own face smiled at me from the front page.

But I wasn't smiling now. It had begun to rain. The water was pattering down on the tin roof like somebody had dropped a bag of marbles. The policeman yawned and turned a page. I shifted in my seat and the handcuffs clinked.

We drove for almost an hour, heading west. Then we slowed down. I saw a gate slide shut behind us. The van stopped. We had arrived.

The prison was an ugly Victorian building: rust-coloured bricks and a grey slate roof. It was shaped like a square with a wall running all the way round and a watch-tower at each corner. The watch-towers were connected to the main building by metal draw-bridges which could be raised or lowered automatically. A glass fronted lodge stood beside the gate. Central control.

I was led in through a door in the side of the prison. And suddenly it was as if I'd stepped off the planet. All the street sounds, even the whisper of the wind, had been cut out. The air smelt of sweat and machine oil. The door clicked shut.

The policemen led me to a counter where a man in guard's uniform was waiting for me.

'Simple?' the guard asked.

'That's him,' the policeman said.

'All right.'

The two policemen left.

I was told to empty my pockets. Everything I owned – even my watch – was taken from me and put in a cardboard box marked with my name. The guard wrote it all down on a sheet of paper.

'Two pounds in loose change. One pen. One lucky rabbit's foot . . .' he smiled mirthlessly, '. . . obviously not working. One bag of salt and vinegar crisps, half eaten. An elastic band . . .'

He made me sign for them, then told me to strip. My clothes went into the box and he handed me a pile of blue denim and white cotton with a pair of boots balanced on the top.

'Now you take a shower,' he said.

'But I've already had a shower.'

'Just do as you're told.'

I took a shower. A medical examination followed. I was poked, prodded and injected. My hair was cut. Finally, I was allowed to dress. The shirt was too small and the boots were too big but somehow I didn't think they were interested in the latest fashion. After that, a second guard appeared. There was a chain looping down the side of his trousers all the way to his knee.

'This way 95446,' he said.

95446 – that was the number stencilled on the front of my new jacket. That was me.

I was taken to the governor's office where a middle-aged man sat writing behind a middle-aged desk. There was a portrait of the Queen on the wall behind him. Even the frame was barred.

'Stand up straight with your legs apart and your hands behind your back while you speak to the governor,' the guard said.

I did as I was told. The governor threw down his pen, looked at me tiredly and began to speak. He must have said the same speech a hundred times before.

'95446,' he began. 'You are here to pay your debt to society. How you pay that debt is up to you. There's the easy way and the hard way. If you obey the rules and cause no trouble . . .'

His voice faded away. I wasn't listening any more. I hadn't really taken anything in from the moment I'd arrived. I could still hear the click of the door and, in the distance, the voice of the judge echoing over and over again, '. . . *you will go to prison for eighteen months* . . .'

Eighteen months! I would be fifteen when I got out, practically middle-aged. I'd never get a job. I'd have to drink tea with social workers. Eighteen months! I'd miss two Cup Finals, seventy-two episodes of the A-team. And what about school? I could kiss goodbye to my O-levels now. Eighteen months! If I tried to mark up the days on the wall I'd run out of wall.

I was still in a daze when the governor finished and I was led back into the main body of the prison.

I hardly saw the corridors stretching down with the cells in two tiers on both sides. I hardly heard the shouts and taunts of the inmates. I hardly felt the shirt slicing into my arm-pits or the boots rubbing blisters on my heels.

I only came to when the guard prodded me into a cell and locked the door behind me. The cell was about twelve feet by six – and whoever had built it had had small feet. Bare bricks, a tiny window, two chairs, a table, a wash basin, a bucket and a pair of bunk beds, one above the other. A figure rolled off the lower bunk and gave me a crooked smile.

'Welcome to Strangeday Hall, kid,' he said. 'I'm Johnny Powers.'

5

Johnny Powers

'Welcome to Strangeday Hall. I'm Johnny Powers.'

The words hadn't been spoken in a friendly way. The voice was cold, mocking – with a twist of Irish in the accent. My cell-mate perched on the edge of the bunk, rolling a cigarette. I looked at him and my mouth went dry. I'd seen some nasties in my time but this guy was something else again.

He was about the same height as me although he was two years older, thickset and fleshy. He had small, ugly eyes, a small, upturned nose and a narrow mouth set in a permanent sneer. He wore his hair greased back, the hair-line snaking across his brow. His skin was pale and lifeless. Maybe he'd spent too much time out of the sun. Or maybe he was already dead but people had been too afraid to mention it to him.

That was the most frightening thing about him – his agelessness. I knew he was fifteen, but he had the face of a baby. Chubby cheeks and perfect teeth. His eye-lashes could have been painted on with a brush. Yet when he smiled (he was smiling at me now) there was suddenly an old man sitting there, an old man who liked killing people. I wondered how many people had left this world with that smile fading in their eyes.

This was Johnny Powers. Public Enemy Number

One. He had hitch-hiked his way out of somebody's nightmare.

'Hi,' I said. 'I'm Nick Simple.'

'Simple – huh?' He licked the cigarette paper and sealed it. 'What are you in for?'

'A jewel robbery,' I said. I was in no mood to explain. 'The Woburn Carbuncles.'

'Is that so?' His eyes twinkled and he looked genuinely pleased. 'Now ya mention it, I remember reading something about it.' The face hardened. 'But just don't get any bright ideas while you're here, kid. I'm number one in this joint. Ya do things my way. Or ya never do nothing again.'

'Sure. Absolutely!'

Well, what else could I say to him? Johnny Powers was obviously so far round the bend that he was coming back round the other side.

I threw my few possessions on to the top bunk. 'What happened to your last cell-mate?' I asked.

Powers smiled his crooked smile. 'He and I didn't get along so good,' he said. 'So one night he jumped out of the window.'

I glanced at the window. 'But it's barred,' I said.

'Yeah. He jumped out one piece at a time.' Powers screwed the cigarette into his mouth. 'Maybe I gave him a little help. Know what I mean?' He giggled. 'Ya need any help, just ask.'

'I'll let you know,' I said.

A bell rang then and the cell door opened. I looked at my watch, remembered it wasn't there and followed Powers out. There were kids streaming out of the cells on both sides of the corridor and above me too. They were all in identical uniforms, the same uniform that I was wearing. None of them were over sixteen. None of them were smiling. There must have been three hundred of them. Three hundred of us. I kept on having to remind myself that I was one of them . . . would be for the next year and a half.

We marched through a door and into a large hall with long tables set in two rows and a balcony at one end where an armed guard stood watching us. A notice hung on one wall: 'Prisoners are forbidden to talk during meal time.' A few minutes later I got my first taste of prison food. Taste is the wrong word. It didn't have any. We lined up at a hatch where we were served watery stew, mashed potatoes and cabbage, prunes and custard. Shut your eyes and you wouldn't know which was which. I didn't like to think what animal had ended its days in the stew. All I can say is that it had a lot of fat, not a lot of meat, and some sort of disease.

Nobody talked and for ten minutes the only sound was the clatter of spoons and forks against tin trays. I didn't eat anything. I'd left my appetite in the number three court of the Old Bailey. It was probably still sitting in the dock, dreaming of a Macdonalds. Another bell rang and we carried the trays back to the hatch. I'd just handed mine over when there was a crackle from a loudspeaker and a voice called out.

'95446 Simple to the visitor's room.'

Powers was right behind me. 'Well whaddya know,' he whispered. 'Only been here five minutes and ya got callers.'

A guard appeared and led me back through the

door, down a corridor, up a flight of stairs and into another room.

'So you finally ended up where you belong,' Chief Inspector Snape said.

Of course I'd expected to see him sooner or later. Snape had set it all up from the start. He'd asked me to share a cell with Johnny Powers and when I'd refused he'd gone ahead and arranged it anyway. He must have found out about the trip to Woburn Abbey. Somehow he'd held the other tourists back so that I'd be in the room with the carbuncles alone. One of his men had already slipped an extra jewel into my jacket pocket. Another had smashed the cabinet. After that I more or less played into his hands – or at least, his handcuffs.

And here he was, sitting at a table, smoking. Boyle stood behind him, grinning at me like he'd just heard some great joke. Only I was the joke. Well, they hadn't heard anything yet. Did they really expect me to take all this sitting down?

'Sit down,' Snape said.

'Snape,' I muttered. 'You're a snape-in-the-grass.'

I didn't really call him that. If I told you what I really called him, they'd never print it.

'Take a seat, laddy,' he replied. 'I can understand you're a bit cut up, but . . .'

'Cut up?' I almost screamed at him. 'What do you mean "cut up"? I've been sent to prison. I've got eighteen months. Eighteen months? I'll be lucky if I manage eighteen minutes! I'm sharing a cell with a loony. And you know what happened to his last cell-mate? Yeah – he was "cut up" all right. Into lots of pieces!'

He waited until I'd finished, then gestured at the chair. Boyle nodded, the smile still on his face. Wearily I sat down.

'I need a job done,' Snape said.

'A job,' Boyle muttered.

'Powers could be the only chance I have of getting to The Fence. I told you I have to find him.'

'And I told you – no!' I sighed. 'You could have found someone else to do it for you.'

Snape shook his head. 'There was nobody else. It had to be you, laddy. You're thirteen, and you're smart. You proved that with the Malteser business. And the trouble is, we don't have much time.'

'Time?' I almost laughed. 'Well, I've got plenty of time. Eighteen months . . .'

Snape shook his head again. 'I'm afraid not. You see I've just got the latest psychiatric reports on Powers.'

'And what do the psychiatrists say?'

'They don't say anything. They're too frightened to be in the same room as him. They won't go anywhere near him. He's violent. Homicidal . . .'

'I had noticed.'

'. . . and he's getting worse. Any day he could crack up altogether. After that he'll be useless to me. A vegetable . . .'

'I don't get the problem,' I said. 'It's never stopped you working with Boyle.'

At least that finally wiped the smile off Boyle's face. He lumbered towards me, his hands outstretched.

'No, Boyle,' Snape sighed.

'I'll kill him . . .'

'No!'

'I'll say it was an accident,' Boyle pleaded. 'I'll say he was resisting arrest.'

'How can he be resisting arrest when he's already in prison?' Snape demanded.

Boyle had no answer to that. He went off to sulk in the corner.

'What was that you were saying about violent and homicidal?' I asked.

Snape glanced at his deputy then turned back to me. 'You have to get the name out of Powers while he can still talk,' he said. 'One name. That's all we want.'

'And what if I refuse?'

He shrugged. 'Then you're here for another seventeen months and thirty days.'

'Wait a minute . . . !'

'No. You wait a minute, laddy.' Snape leant forward across the table. 'Only two people in the world know that you didn't really steal the Woburn Carbuncle. Boyle and me.'

'What about the security guards?'

'You'll never find them. We got you in here. Only we can get you out. But if you refuse to co-operate . . .' He left the sentence hanging in the air. Right then I'd have liked to have seen him hanging in the air beside it.

I stood up.

'The Fence,' I said.

'Get close to Powers . . .'

'Close?' I cried. 'If I got any closer we'd be sharing the same bed.' I took a deep breath. Snape had beaten me and he knew it. 'All right,' I said.

'You win. I'll find out what you want to know. But if you don't get me out of here . . .'

'Relax.' Suddenly Snape was all smiles again. He dug a hand into his pocket and pulled something out. He threw it down on the table. 'Have a bar of chocolate on us, laddy,' he said. 'Boyle and me bought it for you. Thick and nutty.'

'Yeah.' I gazed at the two of them and sighed. 'I couldn't have put it better myself.'

Powers was waiting for me when I got back to the cell. He was rolling another cigarette. He didn't actually smoke them. He just liked rolling them.

'So who was it?' he asked.

'The police,' I said. I'd been practising my answer on the way. 'Seems I hit the old lady harder than I thought. She may bleat.'

'Bleat?'

'I mean . . . croak.' It would take me time to get used to the gangster slang. I sat down at the table and shrugged. 'I guess they were trying to frighten me.'

It was the first time I'd lied to Johnny Powers and he almost seemed to sense it like a dog scenting blood. He looked at me curiously, the skin under his eyes tightening. But he didn't say anything. Not yet. Some time later the lights went out. There was no 'goodnights'. Nobody came to tuck me in. The darkness just cut in without argument. And that was all.

My first night in Strangeday Hall. I undressed and climbed on to the top bunk, pulling the rough blankets and even rougher sheet over me. The pillow was as soft as cardboard. There was a full moon that night, spilling in through the window. A perfect square of light perched on the wall, cut into sections by the black shadows of the bars. In the distance, a plane screamed through the sky.

I lay there for an hour. I couldn't sleep. There was only one way out of this mess and the sooner I started, the better. Cursing Snape, I opened my eyes.

'Powers?' I said.

'Yeah?' He sounded wide-awake too.

'I just want you to know . . . I really admire you. I read about you in all the papers. I always hoped I could join up with you.'

'Is that so?' I couldn't tell if he believed me. His voice was cold, empty.

I swallowed and went on. 'When I stole that jewel . . . I had a catapult in my pocket. Like your gang – The Catapult Kids.'

'We never had no catapults.'

'Sure, Powers. But I couldn't afford a shot-gun. That's why I was stealing the jewel.' There was no answer. 'I'd have got away if you'd been there. And then we could have sold the jewel. It was worth thousands. The only thing is, I didn't know who to sell it to. What would you have done, Powers?'

There was a long silence. I didn't even hear him get out of bed. But a second later he was standing up with his head close to mine, the moon dancing in his eyes.

'Listen, Simple,' he said. 'I don't know ya and what I don't know I don't trust. Maybe you're on the level. If not, ya'll end up six feet underneath it. Know what I mean?'

He stared at me. There was still something of the choirboy in his face. But it was a choirboy who would burn down the church sooner than sing in it.

'Ya want some advice?' he said. 'Act like a shirt.'

'Like a shirt?'

'Yeah. Button it.'

Then he was gone. I turned over and shut my eyes. But the sun was already rising before I got any sleep.

6
Inside . . .

Three weeks after I'd arrived at Strangeday Hall, Herbert sent me a cake. He'd made it himself – with eggs, flour, sugar, a hint of ginger and a Black & Decker electric drill. The drill was buried in the middle. I guess it was his idea of The Great Escape. He needn't have bothered. Hiding a drill in a cake wasn't such a bad thought, but he could have put it in there *after* he'd baked it. By the time it came out of the oven there was as much cake in the drill as there was drill in the cake. And he forgot to enclose a plug.

Mind you, it was about the only good joke in the first month. There I was surrounded by some of the toughest thugs and heavies in the country – people who would break your arms as soon as look at you. And that was just the guards. Most of the inmates were OK although I did have an unfortunate run-in with a pick-pocket. I didn't have any money, of course. But he stole my pockets.

What can I say about life on the inside? Perhaps you've heard that phrase – 'a short sharp shock'. Well Strangeday Hall was more of a long, drawn-out surprise. It was the only prison in England like it. And I can tell you now, I didn't like it at all.

Up at six in the morning. Luke-warm showers – or stone cold if Luke had forgotten to turn the hot water on. Breakfast: a mug of tea, two slices of bread and one slice of porridge. Then work until lunch-time. There were two workshops in the prison. In the first we sewed mail-bags. I was put in the second, assembling dolls for some charity. I must have assembled hundreds of them. After a week I couldn't stand the sight of them. So if you ever get a doll with two fractured knee-caps and the initials NDS scratched across the shoulders, you'll know where it came from.

Lunch was at twelve. Stomach aches were at half-past. After that we were allowed two hours' exercise. Sport was encouraged at Strangeday Hall. But not all sport. Cross-country running, for example, had been crossed off the agenda after the Junior Team made it to Scandinavia during the inter-prison finals. So normally we just walked around the yard. Sometimes the screws made us do army exercises – square bashing – to keep us on our toes. Two hours marching up and down the concrete at double speed and it felt like you didn't have any toes left.

And then there were the exhibition games. Football.

I only ever saw one match. Some London public school – Westminster or Eton – sent in a team of kids to play against us in a 'friendly' match. That was their word, not ours. Well, it was all friendly smiles while they got off the coach. The referee made a nice speech about sportsmanship and fair play. Then the whistle went. Nobody saw where it went. And that was just the start.

Two minutes into the game, our centre half mugged their right wing. By half-time, we'd demoralized their forwards and broken their backs. Our captain tried to blackmail their goalkeeper. Then somebody stole the ball. We won in the end: 6–0. Nobody scored. But that was how many of their side left the field on stretchers.

Anyway, after the physical exercise came the mental exercises. Strangeday Hall had the only classroom I've ever seen where the chalk was chained to the blackboard and the teacher was protected by Alsatian dogs. And the dogs were probably more intelligent than most of the pupils.

We were locked in our cells until tea-time . . . and that was where I'd come in. Tea finished at six-thirty and then we were locked up again until the lights went out at ten. One day in the life of a jail-bird. And I can tell you now, if I'd been sent there for life, I wouldn't have lasted a day.

But I was still working on Johnny Powers, my express ticket out. You'd have thought I'd have been able to get somewhere with him after four weeks in the same cell. But you'd be wrong. He was about as suspicious as a snake in a handbag factory and twice as poisonous. I was playing the tough kid, anxious to learn from him. All I wanted was one name – The Fence. All I got was monosyllables and sneers.

Worse still, he was cracking up fast. He got these headaches. One minute he'd be sitting there vandalizing a good book. The next he'd be curled up with his head in his hands, groaning and sweating. I tried offering him aspirin but he didn't even hear me. That was when I found out about his mother. He might have sold his granny to the salt-mines, but he still loved his mother. He'd call out for her. And hours later, when the headache had gone but she hadn't come, he would sit there, hunched up, sucking his thumb. I could see what Snape meant. Powers needed a new jacket. The sort with the sleeves that button up behind the back. Another few weeks and he'd be swapping his cell for one with padded walls. And where would that leave me?

Everything changed one afternoon. I think it was a Tuesday, but in prison every day is so similar that they don't really need names. I was on cleaning duty. I'd cleaned the kitchen, the dining hall and two corridors and they were still pretty filthy. At Strangeday Hall you could never get rid of the dirt. You could just re-arrange it. It was late in the afternoon and I thought I'd finished, but then one of the screws came up to me. His name was Walsh. We called him 'Weasel' on account of his thin face, his pointed nose and his little moustache. He didn't like me. He didn't much like anyone.

'Finished, 95446?' he asked.

'Yes sir, Mr Walsh.' I smiled at him. 'Why don't you call me 954 for short?' I said. 'It's more friendly.'

He stared at me, his left eye twitching. 'Are you trying to be funny 95446?' he asked.

'No, Mr Walsh.'

'Go and clean the showers. I want them spotless.'

'But Mr Walsh . . .'

'Are you arguing, 95446?'

'No, Mr Walsh.'

Prison officers and teachers have a lot in common.

It must have been about half past four when I set out across the yard to the showers which were in a low building on the other side. All the other inmates were either in the classrooms or locked up in their cells. High above me, the guards looked down from their metal watch-towers, fingering their automatic rifles like I was a duck in a fairground. Scratch one Simple and win a goldfish. I looked up at them and waved. Somebody telephoned the central control lodge and a moment later the door to the shower cubicles clicked open.

A plane passed overhead. It was our only connection with the outside world and most of us would have been glad to lose it. But there was one guy in the cell next to mine who'd made a life study of the flight paths. That's what he'd got – life. He'd burnt down his school. But first he'd disconnected the fire alarms in the staff room. Anyway, he knew every plane just by the sound of its engine. And he'd sit there, gazing up at the ceiling, muttering to anyone who'd listen:

'Four twenty-two, KLM Tri-star to Amsterdam. Four thirty, Singapore Airlines 747 to Singapore. Four thirty-nine, British Airways Concorde to New York . . .'

Poor guy. He had planes on the brain. Another year and he'd be plainly insane.

I went into the showers. The door led into a white-tiled room with hooks and benches where we got undressed. From here a long corridor stretched down to the far wall with metal cubicles on both sides. The cubicles didn't have curtains. There was no privacy at Strangeday Hall. Or maybe someone had stolen them too. The showers were regulated by three huge taps in a maze of pipes, valves and gauges close to the changing room. The whole system must have been out-of-date the day it was built. And that day must have been some time before the Victorians.

I'd thought I'd be alone there but I hadn't taken two steps before I heard voices, low and threatening behind the drip of the water. Carefully, I put down my bucket and mop, then edged towards the corridor. There was something about the voices that I didn't like, and I couldn't even hear what they were saying yet. But nobody was meant to be in the showers. If they'd sneaked in in the middle of the afternoon, it wasn't because they fancied a wash.

I reached the corridor and slipped behind the first of the partitions, next to the taps. From here I could get a better view. With my cheek pressed against the cold metal, I peered round. What I saw was even worse than I'd expected. And at Strangeday Hall expectations were always pretty bad.

Johnny Powers was there, slumped against the far wall. It was difficult to see in the half-light, but I could tell he'd taken a beating. He was sitting like a broken doll. Nobody had scratched their initials into him yet, but his nose was bleeding and for once his hair was ruffled. There were three guys with him. I recognized them at once, even with their backs to me, and my mouth went dry.

The tallest of them was called Mark White – three years for armed robbery. He was the most crooked con in the joint: crooked shoulders, crooked hips and a crooked smile. In a funny way he was quite good-looking, like a male model. But it was like someone had torn him out of a magazine and crumpled him up. He was crooked all over. There was another Mark with him – Mark Hards: two years for cat burglary. All he ever stole was cats. He was small with greasy hair and a pronounced stomach . . . which he pronounced 'stumma'. Half the time you couldn't understand what he was saying. Most of the time you didn't want to. I didn't know what the third guy was in for. He had the unlikely name of Zuckie Hommel. He was blond and ugly. Somebody once told me he'd murdered his dentist. If I'd had teeth like his I'd have probably murdered mine.

'Aren't you going to call for help, Johnny?' White was saying. I could hear them all now. 'Maybe one of the screws will hear you.'

'I don't need help from no one.' Powers spat blood.

'Let him have it,' Hommel hissed. 'Do it now.'

'Yeah – do it now.' Powers giggled. 'Whassa matter, White? Mebbe ya're a bit yellow too. White and yellow – like an egg.'

White moved to one side. That was when I saw what he was carrying. I couldn't believe it. Just about every prisoner at Strangeday Hall had a weapon of some sort, usually home-made daggers or 'shanks' as they were called. But White had gone one better. Somehow he'd got hold of a gun. And he was pointing it at Powers.

'You're going to get it, Johnny,' he said. 'But not yet.' He glanced upwards. 'I reckon you've got another couple of minutes . . .'

Another couple of minutes. My mind was racing. What would happen in another couple of minutes?

Then I remembered. Four thirty-nine. British Airways Concorde to New York. It was the loudest plane of them all. When it passed overhead every afternoon, you couldn't hear yourself talk. Its sonic boom drowned out everything. It would drown out the sound of the gun-shot. It was the perfect cover. Johnny Powers would be drowned and shot at the same time.

If it had been anybody else, I might have just backed out then and there. It was none of my business who was shooting who or why. But this was Powers. If he died, I was finished. Would Snape relent and pull me out if he knew that Powers had taken his secret to the grave? Somehow I doubted it. I'd be left with seventeen months and a criminal record. I had no choice. I had to get Powers out of there – and in one piece.

I looked around me. I don't know what I expected to find. An automatic rifle accidentally left there by one of the guards? If so, I was out of luck. All I could see was a broken shoe-lace and an old towel lying in a puddle of water.

'Two minutes, Johnny,' White said. 'You got any last minute requests?'

'Yeah. Drop dead.' That was typical Powers. If he'd made a request on the radio it would have been for the funeral march.

But looking at the towel had given me an idea. Moving as quietly as I could, I went over and examined the Victorian plumbing system. Three taps – one for hot water, one for cold. The third controlled the pressure. There was a gauge with pipes snaking in and out, a circular clock-face with a big slice of red. I guessed the system had never been turned to full pressure. The whole thing would probably explode.

Well, there was always a first time . . .

I gripped the tap. The metal was cool and damp against the palm of my hand. Hoping it wouldn't squeak, I gave it a quarter turn to the right. There was a loud shudder. The pipes coughed and water gurgled like a man with chronic indigestion.

'Whassat?' Hards asked. He'd heard it too. He'd have had to be deaf to miss it.

'It's nothing,' White replied and I breathed again. 'Just the pipes.'

I turned the tap again. It made two complete revolutions before it tightened, fully open. All the pipes were bubbling and groaning now. I looked at the pressure gauge. The needle had jerked up like a conductor's baton. Already it was vertical and even as I watched it began to shiver towards the right.

'You sure?' Hards asked again. He had a sulky, unhappy voice.

'Go check it out if you're so worried,' White replied.

'I wanna ask ya something,' Powers said suddenly.

Did Powers know I was there? Had he guessed? Or perhaps he'd seen me. He was the only one facing the door. Anyway, he was smart enough to hold their attention. If not, I'd have been found there and we would have both ended up with an extra hole that neither of us needed.

'What is it?' White said.

'Who put ya up to this?' Powers demanded. 'Who sent ya the gun? I'd just like to know.'

'Who do you think?' White asked. There was a pause. 'OK. I'll tell you. It was Big Ed.'

'Big Ed?'

'Yeah. He figured it's time you kinda left the scene. Permanently. Know what I mean?'

'Well, whaddya know?' Powers muttered. 'Big Ed . . .'

'White . . .' Hards began again.

But then he stopped. I could hear another sound now, even louder than the pipes. It was a distant whine getting louder and closer by the second. The four thirty-nine Concorde was dead on time. And time had just run out for Johnny Powers.

'Here it comes,' White said. 'Say your prayers, Johnny.'

I reached for the towel, picked it up, slapped it against the hot tap. Even with the wet material, I could feel the metal burning underneath. The showers might have been luke-warm for us, but right now they were white hot. I glanced at the pressure gauge. The needle had passed right through the red section and was trying to find a way out on the other side. The whine of the plane had become a roar. Any moment now it would become a boom. Clutching the tap through the towel I turned it as fast as I could. Then everything happened at once.

There was a great hiss as the water rushed through the taps. All the showers sprang into life at once, boiling water spraying out in all directions. The pipes rattled and shook like they were trying to tear themselves out of the wall. Steam filled the room, a sudden impenetrable fog.

'What the . . . ?' White began.

Then one of the showers exploded, the spout ricocheting across the room like a bullet. Steam and water bellowed out in a jet. Concorde was right overhead now. The whole building was vibrating. There was a gun-shot. Even at that close range I hardly heard it. Then a second shower blew itself apart, unable to bear the pressure. Zuckie Hommel screamed, his face disappearing in a blast of white heat.

I'd wrapped the towel round my face and I was on my knees, crawling underneath the swirling clouds. I couldn't see anything. I could hardly hear anything. The pipes were slamming against the wall in a frenzy. Three more showers exploded. Burning water cascaded on to my back.

'Johnny!' I called out. My voice was muffled by the towel. There was no reply and I wondered if despite everything he'd been shot. Then there was a splat of fist against flesh and a figure flew through the mist, crashed into a cubicle and slumped beside me. It was White. He was out cold – about the only thing in the building that was cold. He no longer had the gun.

Then somebody else lurched out of the steam on all fours. This time it was Powers. Miraculously, he didn't seem to have been burnt.

'Good work, kid,' he said. There was a glimmer in his eyes and he was smiling. I couldn't think of anything to say. He was actually enjoying all this.

It was over as quickly as it had begun.

The Concorde flew past, trailing its sonic boom with it. The pipes buckled, broke, then fell silent as the pressure went down. Water, suddenly cold, splashed down on the concrete floor. Somewhere in all the steam, Hards groaned. White and Hommel lay still, their bodies vague outlines in the haze. Powers and I crawled back to the door and stood up. Somehow I found the presence of mind to pick up the mop and bucket. I gave Powers the mop. Together we walked back across the yard. The guards didn't try to stop us.

Later I heard that White and Hards had taken the rap for destroying the showers. They both got one month's solitary and the removal of all privileges. Hommel ended up in the prison hospital. He hadn't been pretty to begin with but after his steam shower the only job he'd be getting would be in a horror film. Powers and I were questioned about our part in the affair but we just played dumb. White was in no position to be telling stories.

That night, back in the cell, Powers asked me why I'd saved him.

'I told you.' I shrugged, trying to make nothing of it. 'I admire you. I wasn't going to let those creeps put a bullet in you.'

Powers stood up, holding out a hand. I shook it. And I still had five fingers when he let it go. 'Ya're all right, kid,' he said. 'Ya're OK.'

That was as close as he could get to saying 'thank you'. But I was satisfied as I went to sleep. I'd become his friend, just the way Snape wanted. Surely it could only be a matter of time before I was out of Strangeday Hall.

It was only a matter of time – although things didn't happen quite the way I'd expected. But then, when did they ever?'

7
. . . Out!

The day after the attack in the shower room, Powers got a letter. We received letters twice a week, but only after the governor had censored them. If he didn't like a sentence, he simply took a pair of scissors and cut it out. I got one letter from Herbert that more or less fell apart in my hands. It began 'Dear Nick' and ended 'Your big brother Tim'. The rest was just holes apart from the single word 'peacock' which I found screwed up at the bottom of the envelope. Well, at least that told me he was still looking for the lost Ming vase. Unless, of course, by some miracle he'd already found it.

The letter Powers got had come through uncut. He read it three times, concentrating on every word. Then he paced up and down the cell for an hour. By now I knew enough not to ask any questions. If Powers wanted me to know something, he would tell me. At last he turned round and walked over to the table.

'I'm getting outta here,' he said.

'Out, Johnny?' I didn't know what to say. 'How come?'

'Read this.' He pushed the letter into my hands. I read it.

Johnny –
Bad news I'm afraid. Grandpa's in emergency care,

dear. They're talking of another operation. Kingston Hospital is ready now, but Grandpa's last operation wasn't very successful. Everyone is really upset.

Caroline and Oliver got married in Edinburgh yesterday. He's an optician, and marvellous with eyes. We'll all miss them.

No other important news. Take care.

Yours ever,

Ma.

I finished the letter and glanced up. Powers was staring at me, waiting for me to speak. 'That's bad,' I said.

'Yeah.'

'I mean . . . you must be worried about your grandad, but I don't see . . .'

'My grandad died ten years ago!' He snatched the letter back and spread it out on the table. 'Ya don't understand,' he went on. 'Ma and me have this secret code.'

I read the letter again, but I still couldn't see it.

Powers jerked a thumb towards the page. 'Ya take the first letter of every other word. That way ya get the real message.

I read the letter for a third time, starting with the B of 'Bad'. And at last it made sense.

BIG ED TAKING OVER. COME HOME AT ONCE.

'Big Ed,' I muttered. I'd heard that name only the day before. He'd been the one who'd sent White and the others to deal with Powers.

'Ya can cut London into four slices,' Powers explained. 'North, south, east and west. There's a gang for each slice . . . like, ya know, we got a gentleman's agreement. The east was my territory – until I got slammed up here. Since then, my ma's been looking after it. She's an ace, my ma. Top of the world.

'Now, Big Ed handles the south. That's fine by me. Until he gets greedy. With me outta the way, he thinks maybe he can muscle in on my territory. Only it would be better for him if I was outta the way more permanent like. So he sends White and the others after me. And then he goes gunning after Ma.'

Powers paused and I was amazed to see a tear trickle down one of his pale, choirboy cheeks.

'Ya don't know my ma,' he said. 'She's as tough as old nails. She's a real killer. And her cooking! Nobody makes a moussaka like her – all hot and bubbling with the cheese melted on top. She sent me one here, back in February.'

'The St Valentine's Day moussaka?' I asked.

'That's right. But she's an old lady. She can't stand up to Big Ed on her own. She needs me. That's why she sent me the letter.'

He got up again and went over to the door. For a minute he listened carefully. When he was satisfied that there was no one there, he came back to the table.

'I'm busting outta here,' he said in a low voice. 'And ya're coming with me.'

'That's terrific!' I said. '*This is terrible!*' I thought.

'We'll go together.'

'When? How?'

'Ya leave the thinking to me, kid.'

And that was all he would say.

Another week passed. I assembled another fifty dolls, cleaned plates, washed floors, marched around the yard and fell asleep in class. I heard Zuckie Hommel had got parole and been released from hospital. He left half his face behind him. Powers barely said a word during all this time, but he got two visits from his solicitor. He came back from each visit with a sly, secretive smile and an ugly light in his eyes. Somehow I didn't think they'd been discussing legal niceties. Illegal, more likely, and probably not-very-niceties either.

It all came together one Friday morning, six weeks to the day since my arrival at Strangeday Hall. There were two visiting sessions on Fridays – one in the morning, one in the afternoon. Powers had got a visit from some broad who claimed she was his cousin. If she was his cousin, I was Nick Van Simple, the well-known Dutchman. Powers came back to the cell flushed with excitement. But there was something else too. He was angry, frustrated.

He waited until he was sure nobody was listening. Then he came over and whispered to me. 'It's on,' he said. 'We go tonight.'

'Tonight?'

'That's right, kid. But there's a problem.' He pounded his fist into the palm of his hand. 'Nails Nathan,' he hissed.

'What about him?'

'He's my getaway driver. Only he's sick. He's got food poisoning.' Powers kicked the wall. 'I'll poison him all right . . .'

'Can't we wait until he gets better?' I asked.

'We can't wait. Everything's been set up. We gotta go tonight.' He thought for a minute. 'Wait a minute,' he said. 'Didn't ya say ya brother was visiting ya this afternoon?'

'Yes.'

'Can he drive?'

'Yes. But . . .'

'That's perfect then.' Powers blew on the palm of his hand. 'Tell him he's gotta be at Terminal Two – departures, Heathrow at eleven o'clock tonight.'

'Heathrow?' I stared at him. 'Are we flying out of here?'

'Ya'll see.' Powers gave me another sly smile. 'Just make sure he's there.'

'But Johnny,' I stammered. 'Herbert isn't exactly . . .'

That was as far as I got. Suddenly the smile was gone and the madness was back in his eyes. 'He's ya brother and he can drive. That's all that matters. Don't let me down, kid. I'm counting on ya.'

I could have told him that Herbert was completely incompetent. I could have told him that he'd only passed his driving test after six attempts and that on the fifth attempt he'd run over the driving instructor. I could have added that Herbert was too scared to park on a yellow line, let alone drive a car-load of gangsters out of a maximum security prison. But Johnny Powers was counting on me. If I argued, my number would be up.

'I'll ask him,' I said at last.

'Sure kid. Ask him nicely. And tell him, if he says no . . .' Powers smiled. '. . . the next drive he'll take will be in a hearse.'

* * *

The main prison visiting room was long and narrow, divided in half like two mirror reflections. A row of tables – like small ping-pong tables – ran down the centre. The nets were metal grills. Two doors led into the room: one for inmates, one for visitors. The inmates sat at one end of the tables, the visitors at the other. Nothing was allowed to pass over the grill. You weren't even allowed to shake hands, Two guards stood in the room the whole time, listening to every word that was said.

My problem was that I had to tell Herbert to be at Heathrow airport later that night without telling him why. I knew he'd argue – and probably at the top of his voice. And if the guards overheard anything, that would be that.

He was already sitting there, waiting for me, as I came in. This was his first visit – and he gaped at me like he'd never seen me before. I guessed it was the uniform, the blue denim and stencilled number, that had taken him by surprise. But what had he expected me to be wearing? Top hat and tails? I sat down and for a long time neither of us said anything. Herbert loosened his tie and collar.

'It's like a prison in here,' he said at last.

'It is a prison, Herbert,' I reminded him.

'Oh yes. Yes . . . of course.' He smiled aimlessly. 'How are you?' he asked.

'I'm all right.'

'Well – there's only seventeen months to go. And maybe they'll give you time off for good behaviour. How is your behaviour?'

'It's good,' I said.

'Good.'

There was a long pause. Herbert was obviously lost for words. He'd never had a jail-bird for a brother before and of course he still didn't know that I was innocent. He took out a packet of chewing-gum and offered it to me.

'No passing food over the table,' one of the guards snapped.

'Can I pass it under the table?' Herbert asked.

'No food,' the guard said.

Herbert shrugged, rolled up a piece for himself and flicked it towards his mouth. It missed and hit him in the eye. I sighed. 'How are Mum and Dad?' I asked.

'I called them in Australia,' Herbert said. 'They didn't take the news very well, I'm afraid. Mum had hysterics. Dad disowned you.'

There was another long silence. So much for family loyalty.

Herbert looked at his watch. 'I haven't got long,' he said.

'How's the plane-spotting going, Herbert? I blurted out.

'The plane-spotting?' He looked at me as if I'd gone mad.

'Sure.' One of the guards was listening, obviously puzzled. I smiled at him. 'Some people spot trains,' I said. 'My big brother spots planes.'

'But . . .' Herbert began.

'Seen any good Jumbos lately?' I was smiling frantically now. The guard looked the other way. I winked at Herbert. 'Didn't you say you were going to Heathrow at eleven o'clock tonight? To the departure lounge in Terminal Two?'

I was still winking furiously. 'Have you got something in your eye?' Herbert asked.

'That's right.' I laughed. 'Maybe when you get to Terminal Two at eleven o'clock tonight you can get me some ointment.'

'But Nick . . .'

There was nothing else to do. I stretched under the table and kicked him as hard as I could. Too hard. Herbert screamed. Both the guards hurried over to us.

'What's the matter?' one of them asked.

'It's nothing,' I said. 'My brother was just doing an impersonation. He was taking off a 747. You know . . . a 747 taking off.'

'My ankle!' Herbert moaned.

'That's right,' I continued desperately. 'His uncle. He's hurt his uncle by refusing to take him plane-spotting to Heathrow Airport tonight.'

By now everyone in the room was looking at us. The two guards shook their heads. 'Visiting time over,' one of them said.

I stood up and followed the other inmates through the door and into the prison. Herbert sat where he was, rubbing his ankle and gazing after me. I must have given him quite a bruise. I just hoped he'd got the message.

When you're doing time, time passes slowly. But the rest of that afternoon dragged past like a dying man. At last the sun collapsed behind the prison walls and darkness came. Johnny Powers had barely said a word since I'd got back from the visiting room. I'd told him that I'd got the message across and that Herbert would be there.

'OK, kid. We move at twelve.'

He spoke the words without moving his lips and I remember thinking he'd have made a great ventriloquist. And now that he had Herbert on the payroll, he wouldn't even need to buy a dummy.

Would Herbert show up? That was the question I asked myself over and over again. What would happen if he didn't? I didn't ask that too often. I had visions of myself splattered across the courtyard. If the guards didn't get me, Powers would.

We went down to tea. I couldn't eat a mouthful. Then it was back into the cells and lock-up. Powers dozed off. I lay on my bunk, mentally composing my will. Herbert would get my books, my records and my old stamp collection. I'd leave Snape and Boyle my Australian Y-fronts. *We move at twelve.* How would Powers even know when twelve had arrived? We didn't have a watch. And what was he planning anyway? There were at least four locked doors between us and the main gate. If we climbed the walls we would be too high up to drop down on the other side. And then there were the guards in the watch-towers.

A plane grumbled across the sky. Powers' eyes flickered open.

He didn't say anything. He rolled over and reached underneath the mattress. A moment later he was standing up, the cold moonlight slashing across his face. His eyes were black. There was no colour in his skin. The moonlight glinted off the gun he now held in his right hand. The gun from the shower room. He was only fifteen years old but somehow he was already dead. A discarded frame from one of those old black and white gangster films.

He turned to me.

'It's twelve o'clock, kid,' he said. 'Time to go.'

8
Over the Wall

'What do we do, Johnny?'

'Get on ya bunk. Put ya hands on ya stomach. And start groaning,' he said.

I hesitated for about half a second. Just long enough for him to turn round and hiss 'Move it!' Then I clambered up, curled into a ball and began to groan like I was about to throw up. Which, in fact, I was. I always feel a little queasy when I'm afraid and right now I was scared out of my mind. I knew what Powers was going to do now. I reckoned he was out of his mind too.

He glanced back at me, winked and began to hammer on the door. I could hear the sound echoing down the corridors. There were heavy foot-steps on the cat-walk, coming our way. 'Guard!' Powers shouted. 'Guard!' One of the other prisoners yelled something out. Then there was a rattle of keys and the door swung open. I groaned louder. Powers took a step back.

Walsh was on duty that night. I could just see him out of the corner of my eye, framed in the soft yellow light of the doorway. 'What's the matter, 00666?' he asked.

'It's the kid,' Powers said. 'He's sick.'

After the shower room affair, Walsh didn't trust either of us. I thought for a moment he was going to walk away. I gave a ghastly croak and shuddered.

It wouldn't have won me any major acting awards, but it seemed to convince Walsh. He walked past Powers, further into the cell, and stood beside me. Powers made a sign at me as he edged towards the door. The meaning was clear. Keep Walsh talking.

'I'm sick,' I moaned. 'Something I ate . . .'

'How long have you felt sick?' he asked.

'I've been sick since six. Like 62426.'

'62426?'

'Yeah – he's been sick too. Far too sick.'

'Far too sick for what?'

'Far too sick to eat. So was 42628.'

'42628 was far too sick to eat?'

'No. 42628 ate. But 62426 was far too sick.'

I don't know if Walsh understood a word I was saying. I'm not sure I understood it myself. But while I'd held his attention, Powers had looked up and down the corridor, checking there was no one else around. As Walsh straightened up, he moved. Suddenly the gun was pressed against his neck and Powers was right up close to him, purring like a kitten. A rabid kitten.

'Weasel Walsh,' he muttered. 'Make one false move and I'll decorate the walls with ya brains.'

'Powers!' The colour had drained out of Walsh's face. 'Are you crazy?'

'Sure.' Powers laughed. 'That's what my doctors say. But I ain't so crazy about this joint, Walsh. That's why ya're going to be my ticket out.' He jerked his head towards the door. 'Check it again, kid,' he said. I went over and looked out. The narrow corridor seemed to stretch into infinity, the dull yellow bulbs throwing sticky pools of light on to the floor.

'It's clear, Johnny,' I said.

'Let's go!' Powers pushed Walsh towards me. 'Ya try anything Walsh and it's pop goes the weasel.'

We stepped into the corridor. It's a strange thing about prison. After a while you get used to being locked up. To me it felt all wrong being outside the cell in the middle of the night. The silence was like a physical force. The shadows seemed to reach out as if to grab me. Everything was somehow too big. I could hear my heart pulsing in my ears and the hair on my forehead was damp with sweat. I wanted to go back. I wanted to hear the cell door slam shut behind me. Now I knew what our hamster must have felt like when it went walkabout one Christmas.

Four doors stood between us and the main gate. We'd reached the last one before we were discovered. Walsh had opened the first three without any problem. But as he turned the key in the fourth, the sirens screamed and the whole world went crazy.

We'd climbed a flight of stairs and we were high up. We were also outside. The cold night air came at me in a rush. The sirens were everywhere, ripping into the night. Somebody switched on a spotlight. I saw a perfect circle of light glide across the courtyard far below us then ripple along the wall, counting the bricks. Then it hit us. For a horrible moment I was completely blind. It was a brilliant, exploding blindness. I thought I was going to fall but Powers must have reached out and grabbed me because I felt myself pulled back, my shoulders slamming into the wall behind me.

The fourth door led nowhere. We were on a small platform, about thirty feet above the ground, the same height as the wall. The platform was directly opposite one of the watchtowers. I could just make out the shape of two guards behind the curtain of light. They were pointing something at us – something long and thin. Somehow I didn't think it was a telescope. Sitting ducks. I waited for the crackle of gun-fire that would bring it all to an end.

But it didn't come. Instead the sirens ended, abruptly fading into silence. Now I could hear people shouting. About half a dozen guards ran into the yard, making for the shadows. I looked at Powers. Did he have any idea how he was going to get us out of here? He'd told Herbert to go to Heathrow. I gazed up at the sky almost expecting to see a helicopter – but that was insane. Powers wanted a driver, not a pilot. So what happened next?

'Listen to me!' Powers shouted. 'Do what I tell ya and nobody gets hurt.'

'Put down the gun and give yourself up, Powers.' I don't know who said that. It was just a voice out of the darkness.

'I got nothing to lose,' Powers called back. 'If I don't get some action, Walsh here takes a dive.' He pushed Walsh to the very edge of the platform. I had to admit, he knew what he was doing. If anybody took a pot shot at him now, the guard would fall. 'Lower the drawbridge,' Powers yelled. 'Do it now!'

I'd fogotten the drawbridge. Each watchtower was connected to the prison by a strip of metal that could be lowered or raised automatically. That was why Powers had taken us up and not down into the yard. But would they lower it for him? I'd no sooner asked myself that than there was a low hum and a rectangular shape pushed through the spotlight towards me. So long as Powers held Walsh, he held all the cards.

The drawbridge connected with the platform and the way ahead was clear. I looked at Powers. He was grinning from ear to ear like a kid in a funfair.

'All right,' he shouted at the two guards in the watchtower. 'Drop ya weapons and come over here. But slowly. And no tricks.'

The guards did as they were told and half a minute later there were five of us up there, crowded together in the narrow space.

'You'll never get away with this, Powers,' one of them said.

'No? Just watch me. Come on, kid . . .'

Well, I suppose it was nice that somebody had remembered me. Up to now it had been as if nobody had noticed that I was escaping too. Holding Walsh between us, Powers and I shuffled over to the watchtower and went inside.

'Raise it!' Powers hissed.

Walsh reached out and flicked a switch. The drawbridge swung up again.

So there we now were, cut off in the watchtower with the wall right beside us and a window leading out. But we were still in the prison. If we jumped from the window we'd be lucky to escape with just a broken leg. We wouldn't escape at all. It was a thirty-foot drop and the road running alongside the prison was 100% concrete.

'You can't get down from here, Powers,' Walsh said, echoing my thoughts exactly.

'Ya think so?' Powers glanced in my direction. 'See anything, kid?'

I looked back out of the window. And there was something. I'd never seen anything like it. It wasn't a car. It wasn't a lorry. It was a long rectangular box, riding fifteen feet above the ground. It was held up on hydraulic arms, the wheels far below. Four mattresses had been strapped to the roof. It was driving down the road at about fifteen miles an hour. And it was coming towards us.

'It's coming, Johnny,' I said – even though I didn't know what 'it' was.

'Here's something to remember me by, Weasel,' Powers snarled. He'd turned the gun round in his hand and before either of us could react he brought it crashing down. Walsh crumpled. I was relieved to see he was still breathing. I'd never liked him much. But he was just an ordinary screw doing his job.

I went back to the window. The platform was getting closer. 'We jump?' I asked.

'Ya've hit the nail on the head, kid,' Powers said.

I took one last look at Walsh. 'Yeah . . . and you've hit the screw on the head,' I muttered.

We climbed out of the window and hung there awkwardly. There was no sound from inside the prison. Nobody could see us. Perhaps they didn't realize what we were about to do. The lorry or whatever it was veered towards us without slowing down. Close to, it seemed to be going much faster than I'd thought and whoever was driving it clearly wasn't too sure of himself. It was wobbling all over the place, the tyres thumping into the kerb. At one point it swerved away and I was afraid it was going to miss us altogether. But then it veered back again.

'Now!' Powers shouted.

We dropped.

It was still a long way to fall. It felt like I was in mid-air for ever, like Alice on her way to Wonderland. I heard the engine roaring in my ears. Then I hit the mattress, rolled over, scrabbled for a handhold, somehow managed to cling on. It was a heavy landing. I didn't break any bones, but I must have broken a few springs.

Powers was beside me. 'Move inside,' he said.

The platform was still zig-zagging down the road. Not exactly break-neck speed – unless, that is, you fell off. It was still a long way to fall. With the wind blowing in my hair, I crawled along the roof to the back end. There was a square opening beneath me and I could see lights inside. The wheels hit the kerb again, sending a dustbin flying. Gritting my teeth, I grabbed hold of the edge and heaved myself into space. Now I was hanging there with the road sweeping away behind me. I tried to swing into the box. Then a strong pair of hands reached out and took hold of me. I was pulled inside, dropping the last few feet on to the floor. I stood up and blinked. And only then did I realize what get-away vehicle we were getting away in.

If you've ever been to an airport you may have seen them. They're called 'People movers' or something like that. Imagine an ordinary airport bus, only with more seats and bright neon lights. Then put metal arms between the wheels and the undercarriage. When you step out of the plane, you're about fifteen feet off the ground. But you don't need steps. The driver simply parks the people-mover beside the plane, presses a button and the whole thing rises into the air until it's level with the door. You step inside. The bus sinks back down on to the wheels. And you speed away to the arrival lounge where, provided your driver isn't Herbert Timothy Simple, you finally arrive.

But our driver was Herbert. I could see him at the far end of the bus, sitting in a sort of miniature cubicle, surrounded by switches and levers. He was making the most peculiar noises, whimpering and squeaking with every turn of the wheel.

'Johnny-boy!' a voice said behind me.

I turned round. Powers had followed me into the people-mover and now he was gazing at the man who had pulled us in. Only it wasn't a man. It was a woman. And I didn't need to ask her name to know who she was.

Ma Powers. Johnny's mother.

At first sight she was like any other mother. She was about fifty, wearing a severe black skirt, a matching jacket and a flowery shirt buttoned at the neck. Her hair was grey, mainly hidden by a black velvet hat. Her only make-up was a dash of red lipstick across her tight-lipped mouth. For jewellery she wore plain gold earrings and a cameo brooch in the shape of a rose.

But unlike any other mother, she was carrying a sub-machine gun, the barrel slanting across her chest. The more I looked at her, the less I liked her.

Her eyes – like Johnny's – were two bullet holes in a refrigerator door. She had a tough, weathered face, and when I say weathered I'm talking storms and blizzards. Her skin hung in wrinkles as if it had come unglued from the bones. Her teeth when she smiled, which wasn't often, were yellow and crammed together uncomfortably like a tube train in the rush hour.

'How ya doing, Johnny?' she asked. She spoke just like him, only her voice was deeper.

'I'm OK, Ma,' Powers said. 'All the better for seeing you.'

'That ya friend?' She nodded at me.

'That's right, Ma. Nick . . . come and meet my ma.'

'Not now, Johnny-boy. We gotta move.'

Even as she spoke, I heard the scream of approaching police cars. Looking through the open end of the bus, I could see the flash of blue lights in the distance. Herbert groaned. We were still only doing twenty miles an hour. At that speed, they'd catch up with us in seconds.

'Go and check with ya brother,' Ma Powers commanded. 'I'll hold 'em off.' She cocked the machine gun and moved to the back.

'Has Nails fixed the bus?' Powers asked.

'Sure, Johnny-boy. Bullet-proof windows. Sawn-off back. And a souped-up engine.' She glared at me. 'Shame we ain't got a souped-up driver. Tell him to put his foot down.'

Powers and I ran up to the front of the bus. Herbert was white-faced, his eyes staring, his hands clutching the steering-wheel like he was trying to pull it apart.

'Nick . . . !' he began when he saw me.

'Not now, Herbert,' I said.

'Can't ya lower this thing?' Powers rapped. We were still fifteen feet off the ground, higher than the top deck of a London bus. Only there was no bottom deck.

'I don't know how it works,' Herbert whimpered.

'Didn't Ma show ya?'

'Yes. But I've forgotten.'

'Take the next turning on the left!' Ma Powers called out. Herbert put his foot down and swung the wheel to the left. The people-mover surged forward with fresh power, skidding round the corner. For a horrible moment we were driving on two wheels and I thought the whole thing would topple over. But then it somehow managed to right itself. 'Lower the bus!' Ma Powers shouted.

'Lower the bus!' I screamed.

I'd seen it the moment we'd turned the corner. A road-sign in a red triangle: low bridge ahead, clearance ten feet. About five feet too low. Herbert had seen it too. He took his foot off the accelerator and at once we slowed down. There was a chatter of machine-gun fire from the back of the bus.

'Keep moving!' Ma Powers yelled.

She was cradling the machine-gun like a bouquet of flowers. Except that I've never seen a bouquet with smoke curling out of the end. Looking past her I saw that the first of the police cars had reached the turning. Despite our souped-up engine, it was gaining on us. And there were four more right behind it.

'What do I do?' Herbert moaned.

'Just keep going – fast,' Powers said. Herbert was about to argue but there was something in Johnny's tone of voice that made him think again. He gave a little squeak and stamped down on the accelerator. We rocketed forward.

The machine-gun chattered again. The road was narrow now, hemmed in on both sides by a wire fence. There was only one way to go – and that was straight ahead. But there was the bridge. It was looming up at us, a hump-back bridge with a railway line on top. I could see the rails. I was actually looking down at them. At the rate we were going, we would hit it in around thirty seconds. The metal box of the people-carrier would crash right into the brickwork. I didn't like to think what would happen to the people inside.

Powers ran back to join his mother – perhaps to warn her. I stood beside Herbert, fighting to keep my balance as we bounced over the tarmac, hurtling towards the bridge. He wasn't even trying to lower the bus. He was too frightened to let go of the steering wheel. Desperately I examined the controls. Why did there have to be so many levers? Ma Powers fired for the third time. And this time she found her target. The siren of the nearest police car died away. There was a screech of tyres, a shattering of metal, then an explosion. The bridge glowed red. Twenty seconds until impact.

I ran my hands over the controls, frantically flicking switches and pulling levers left right and centre. I turned out the lights, opened and closed the doors, lowered the aerial and adjusted the mirrors. But I didn't lower the bus. Behind us, Powers was shooting with the pistol he'd taken from the prison. Mother and son seemed to be having a whale of a time. A second police-car had moved up to take the position of the first. And now they were firing too. I tugged at another lever. The ashtray popped out of the dashboard. Ten seconds until impact.

The bridge was right in front of me now, filling up the windscreen. Herbert was whispering something. I think it was a prayer. I slammed my hand down on the controls. My palm hit the black ball at the end of the lever, shifting it forward. I heard a hiss underneath me. The hydraulic arm had come into operation. At the same moment, the whole bus began to sink like the end of a ride in a fun-fair.

But would it sink in time? There were only a few seconds left.

'Brake, Herbert!' I shouted.

We hit the bridge.

We were just low enough to squeeze through. It could only have been a matter of inches. In fact it was only inches. The mattresses didn't make it. I heard them as they were torn free from their bindings and dragged along the roof. Looking back, I saw them plummet into the road behind us, right in the path of the leading police-car. It swerved to avoid them, mounted the kerb and crashed through the fence, finally crushing itself against a lamp-post. Ma Powers gave a short bray of laughter.

'Good work, kid,' Johnny called out.

But it wasn't over yet. We'd taken out two of the five police-cars. That still left three and already they were moving up on us. Ma Powers let off a hail of bullets. I heard a windscreen shatter but they kept on coming. Two of them surged ahead. One stayed behind to keep the back of the bus covered.

The road was wider now. The two police-cars had edged forward and separated so there was one on each side with us sandwiched in the middle.

'Nick . . .' Herbert muttered.

There wasn't much traffic about at that time of night, but looking ahead I saw a lorry thundering towards us. But with the two police cars on either side, we were taking up all the road. Somebody would have to give.

The lorry gave. At the last second, with its headlights dazzling us and the blast of its horn deafening us, it swerved away, left the road and jack-knifed into a field. The lorry had been carrying eggs. I know because some of them splattered into our windscreen. With the horn still blaring, the lorry hit a tree-stump, somersaulted and burst into flames. Later I heard that nobody had been killed. But between us we cooked up a fifty thousand egg omelette.

We were doing nearly seventy miles an hour now. Ahead of us, cars were vacating the road as fast as they could – and they didn't seem to care where they ended up. But they weren't our problem. We were down at ground level. The two police-cars were only inches away, racing alongside us. They had rolled down their windows. Two shot-guns were pointing at us, one on each side. Two blasts and

Herbert and I would have more holes than a colander. We couldn't slow down, not with the third police-car behind us. We were going as fast as we could. We were stuck.

I stared at the nearest policeman, watched his finger tighten on the trigger. For a moment our eyes met and we were trapped in a blue and white nightmare. There was nothing I could do. Nothing? At the last second I slammed my hand down on the controls. The bus rose in the air again. Simultaneously, the two shot-guns fired. But now we were above them. The bullets passed underneath us. The police-car on the left hit the one on the right. The police-car on the right shredded the tyres of the one on the left. Both cars went careering off in opposite directions.

Four down. One to go.

But it seemed that I'd pushed the lever a little too hard. Something had short-circuited. We were no sooner up at the end of the hydraulic arms than we were on the way down again. And that was how we continued, up and down like some crazy jack-in-the-box.

'What are ya doing?' Powers called out.

'It's broken,' Herbert said.

That was the understatement of the year. Sparks were flashing all over the control box. There was a smell of burning rubber and a wisp of smoke crawled into the air. Up and down. I could feel my stomach protesting. It was trying to go the other way.

Then the fifth police-car pulled out and began to overtake. It was the last one left and perhaps the driver thought he could cut us off. Ma Powers opened her handbag, pulled out a spare carbine and reloaded the machine-gun. Johnny followed her as she staggered forward to get a better aim. The control box was on fire now. The engine was howling at us to stop. The hydraulic arms were creaking and shuddering as they pumped us madly up and down. I reckoned we had only a few minutes left before the whole thing either broke down or blew up.

Those last few minutes happened very quickly.

One moment we were up. The next we were at the same level as the police-car. It was edging ahead of us, about to overtake. Ma Powers raised the machine-gun. Then I saw the two passengers in the back seat.

'No!' I shouted.

It was Snape and Boyle. I had no idea what they were doing there. Had they been on the way to the prison when the escape began or was it just a wild coincidence? But it was definitely them. I could even swear that Snape winked at me before Ma Powers opened fire. But I was still shouting when the machine-gun drowned me out. I saw the windows of Snape's car frost over in a thousand cracks. I saw the tyres cut to ribbons. I saw the mirrors and door-handles spin away into the night. The car veered into us, out of control, then swung away. I watched it spiral into the kerb. Then it was as if somebody had picked it up and thrown it. It took off, bounced, cartwheeled into a telephone box. A few seconds later it exploded.

They were dead. Snape and Boyle were dead. There was no way they could have survived. And they were the only people in the world who knew that I'd been framed. They were my only way out of this mess. And they were dead.

I could have cried. But I didn't have time.

There was a sharp bend in the road. I heard Herbert cry out. I looked up. He was spinning the wheel desperately. But we were going too fast. He'd lost control. Ma Powers dropped the machine-gun. Johnny swore. The people-mover, at ground level, left the road, sliced through a hedge and hurtled towards a building. Herbert didn't even have time to slam on the brakes. Travelling at seventy miles an hour we smashed into the wall.

At least, the wheels did. But by the time the impact came, the hydraulic arms had lifted us up again. The wheels, the engine and the undercarriage flattened themselves against solid brick. But the bus itself was fifteen feet up, the same height as the first floor. And on the first floor there was a plate glass window.

The force of the impact tore the bus off the hydraulic arms. As the petrol tank ignited and the undercarriage erupted in flame, the bus itself came free, rammed itself through the window and slid along the floor of the building. The building was an empty office block. There was nothing inside to stop our progress. Carried by our own velocity, we slid the full length of the floor and then – with another explosion of breaking glass – exited through a second window on the other side.

This is it, I muttered to myself as we rocketed out. Now we've got to die.

But the office block looked out over the River Thames. We landed, not with a crash but a splash.

And when I finally found the courage to open my eyes, we were floating gently on the water. We were bruised, shaken and exhausted. But we were still alive.

We floated the rest of the way. There were roadblocks all over London, but we sailed right past them. Nobody had thought to contact the river police. I was free. Over the wall. But Snape and Boyle were dead.

So what did I do next?

9
Wapping Lies

It's funny how often the River Thames seems to feature in my life. When I was chasing the Falcon's Malteser, I was locked up beside it and almost drowned in it. The next time you take a pleasure boat down from Charing Cross pier, look out for a kid dressed in jeans and a baggy sweater floating face-down in the dirty water. It'll probably be me.

The river took us all the way to Wapping. It's just as well the tide was going in our direction or we'd have been out of London via Windsor and on our way to Wales. Even so it was quite a journey. Under Vauxhall Bridge and down past the Houses of Parliament, Somerset House and the National Theatre. Then round the corner and on past Traitor's Gate and the Tower of London, the redeveloped St Katherine's Dock and almost as far as the Isle of Dogs. Dawn was breaking by the time we arrived. By then we'd lost the tourist traps and fancy houses. Or perhaps it was they who had lost us.

This was East London, the heart of Johnny's criminal empire. And looking at it in the cold half-light of the early morning, he was welcome to it.

Everything was grey: the sky, the water, the broken hulks of the old barges moored along the banks. The south side of the river was long and flat, punctuated by a tangle of cranes here, a gas pile there, in the distance a forlorn church steeple.

We moored on the north side at a jetty between two warehouses. There was nobody around. There had probably been nobody in those warehouses for fifty years. A derelict houseboat stood firm a few yards away, tied to the bank and somehow resisting the chop and swell of the Thames water. Shivering, we pulled ourselves out of the broken people-carrier and stood on damp – if not quite dry – land. Ma Powers wanted to sink it, but that wasn't possible. Instead we pushed it back out in mid-stream and let the tide take it on towards the flood barrier and eventually out into the North Sea.

'Where do we go now?' I asked.

'Home,' Ma Powers said. Her lips were set in a frigid scowl. Either it was the cold or she didn't like me. Possibly both.

'East London,' I muttered. 'I'd have thought that was the first place the police would expect us to go.'

'Sure.' Johnny slapped me on the back. 'So it's the last place they'll come looking.'

With Herbert bringing up the rear, we hurried off the jetty and between the warehouses to Wapping High Street. And if this was the high street, I'd hate to see what the low street looked like. It was a spider's web of rusting metal with cranes and scaffolding everywhere. Half the buildings had fallen down. Half of them had only been half-built. It was hard to tell which was which. A patchwork of corrugated iron filled in the gaps, old posters clinging on with tattered fingers. There were no pavements. You couldn't see where the road ended and the gutter began.

We passed through the wreckage for about fifty

yards until we reached another road running off at right angles. There was a barrier across it with a big sign in red and white: ROAD CLOSED. It was blocked by a slanting wall of scaffolding holding up a row of dirty, decrepit houses. We stopped beside the fourth house. Ma Powers fumbled in her handbag and pulled out a set of keys. She turned one in the lock and we went in. We were home.

Johnny Powers needed somewhere to hole up for a while and he'd chosen a real hole. The house was three storeys high, only the third storey had collapsed in on itself. The ground floor was one big room with a couch, a table and chairs, a TV set and an open plan kitchen. It had been a closed plan kitchen until the dividing wall had fallen over. Two doors led out – one to a toilet, the other to a bedroom. There were two more bedrooms and a bathroom upstairs. You could see the bath through a hole in the ceiling.

'Home sweet home,' I muttered.

'It's safe,' Ma Powers said.

'Safe?' I tapped the mantelpiece. A piece fell off. 'You could have fooled me.'

'The police won't come looking for us here,' Johnny said. 'That's what Ma means.'

'What about the neighbours?'

'There are no neighbours,' Ma Powers growled. 'All the houses are condemned.'

'Yeah – and sentenced and executed too,' I said.

Johnny turned to his mother and smiled. 'Ya made it real nice, Ma,' he purred.

I suppose she had done her best to make it comfortable. There were fresh flowers on the table and home-made cushions on the couch. A circular rug lay on the floor, a few pictures hung on the walls and she'd covered the windows with net curtains. But it was like rearranging the cutlery after the Titanic had gone down. The whole place was a disaster. Dry rot, rising damp, woodworm, mould . . . the building would have given a surveyor a field day. Sneeze and a field would be all that was left.

The door to the bedroom opened and another guy walked in. He was about the same age as Johnny, thin and with so much acne you could have struck a match on him. This had to be Nails Nathan. He was biting them even as he walked in. In fact he'd bitten them so far down that he'd started on the fingers. Another few months and they'd have to re-christen him Knuckles Nathan.

'So you made it, Johnny,' he said, smiling nervously and blinking.

'Sure I made it.' Johnny advanced on him. 'But no thanks to you, ya sap.'

'I'm sorry, Johnny.' Nails was whining now. He ran his teeth down the side of his thumb and bit at his wrist. 'I was sick. I couldn't drive.' He paused hopefully. 'But I fixed the car up for you. I did that.'

'You did good, kid.' Johnny gave him a friendly punch in the stomach. Nails doubled up. 'Now fix us some breakfast. And make sure the coffee's good and strong.'

Herbert had been watching all this standing beside the front door. He hadn't said a word which was probably the best thing he could have done. But now he sort of staggered forward and sat down heavily at the table. So heavily that another chunk fell off the mantelpiece.

'I don't believe this,' he said.

'Who is this guy, Johnny-boy?' Ma Powers demanded. She was propping up the machine-gun in the corner like it was a walking stick and she'd just come back from an amble in the park. 'I met him at the airport like ya told me, but I couldn't get no sense outta him. He went on . . . something about plane-spotting.'

Johnny laughed and rolled himself another cigarette. 'Ma,' he said, 'ya ain't met my friend Nick Simple. He saved my life back in the slammer. That's his big brother Herbert?'

'Herbert?' Ma Powers looked at him suspiciously. 'What do you do for a living, Herbert?'

'I'm a private investigator,' Herbert said.

There was a long silence. Nails Nathan dropped a plate. Johnny stared. Right then you could have cut the atmosphere with a knife. Right then I could have cut Herbert with a knife. Why had he had to tell them that? Why couldn't he say he was a chartered accountant or a postman or a brain surgeon or something? Snape had told me that Johnny Powers hated policemen. I somehow guessed he wasn't exactly wild about detectives either.

'A private investigator?' he repeated, his eyes narrowing.

'That's right,' I cut in quick before anyone could say another word. 'Herbert investigates . . .' Nails had turned on a tap to fill the kettle and it was still running. '. . . water! He's a private investigator of water.'

'What is there to investigate about water?' Ma Powers demanded.

'All sorts of things,' I said. 'The amount of chlorine. The bacteria. The . . . um . . . the H.'

'The H?'

'Yeah – you know. Water is H_2O. Herbert has to make sure there's enough H. He works for the Thames Water Authority.'

'OK.' Ma Powers shook her head slowly. 'Maybe that explains why he's such a drip.'

The ice had been broken – or at least, the water. Nails laid the table and we sat down to a breakfast of bacon sandwiches, strong coffee, Shredded Wheat and grapefruit yoghurt. The last two had been suggested by Ma Powers. Without the machine-gun she was just like anyone's mother. I think I preferred her with it.

'Ya don't look so good, Johnny-boy,' she said. 'Did ya eat proper food in prison?'

'Sure, Ma . . .'

'Plenny of fruit? Here – have some grapefruit yoghurt.'

'I'm OK, Ma . . .'

'Do ya want Mummy go get ya some sugar?'

'Ma . . .'

'Yoghurt's good for you, Johnny,' Nails chipped in, spooning out some of his own.

He should have kept his mouth shut. Johnny suddenly picked up his carton and slammed it into Nathan's face, crumpling it against his cheek. Grapefruit yoghurt dripped over his chin and on to his shirt. Ma Powers raised her eyebrows but said nothing. Herbert sighed and reached for the Shredded

Wheat. He wasn't looking too good. I guess his nerves were pretty shredded too.

But at least Johnny cheered up a few minutes later when he finished his coffee and turned on the television. Breakfast TV had just started and the first thing he saw was his own face, a police mug-shot taken a few months before.

'. . . a daring escape from Strangeday Hall late last night. Powers, who was serving fifteen years for armed robbery, is described by the police as unpredictable and extremely dangerous. The public is warned not to approach him.

The picture flickered off to be replaced by the newscaster. He was looking out of the screen with tired eyes, trying not to yawn.

'Accompanying Powers in the break-out was thirteen-year-old Nicholas Simple . . .'

And there I was suddenly on TV. It was the same photograph that had appeared in all the newspapers. Young, innocent, smiling . . . you couldn't believe all the things the newscaster was saying about me.

'Simple, arrested only a month ago following the brutal Woburn Carbuncle robbery, is described as violent and ruthless. In fact if Johnny Powers is Public Enemy Number One, Simple must now be considered Public Enemy Number Two.

'Police are still looking for Herbert Simple, his elder brother, who may be able to help them with their enquiries.'

Johnny switched off the set.

'They're looking for me!' Herbert moaned. He was staring at the blank screen as if the newscaster was about to climb out and grab him.

'Of course they're looking for ya.' Johnny grinned at me. 'Public Enemy Number Two! Ya moved up in the charts pretty quick – eh, kid?'

'Yeah.' I tried to look delighted. It wasn't easy. 'What happens next, Johnny?'

'Right now ya get some sleep. I reckon we could all do with some shut-eye. Isn't that right, Ma?'

'That's right, Johnny-boy.'

'Meantime, Nails can go out and get the rest of the boys together. I'll see them at four. So Nails . . . ya better get a box of cup-cakes or something.'

'Sure thing, Johnny.'

'Good.' Johnny patted me on the shoulder. 'Public Enemy Number Two? I like that, kid. It suits ya.'

At last Herbert and I were alone.

We were sharing a bedroom on the second floor. It was about as comfortable as the living room. There were two single beds leaning unsteadily towards each other, a chair with three legs and a wardrobe minus the door. The window looked out on to a building site behind the house, only there was so much dirt on the glass you could barely see anything.

For a long time neither of us said anything. Herbert looked exhausted. His face was streaked with dust and his hair was standing on end.

'How could you do it, Nick?' he said at last. 'My own brother! First the robbery . . . and then this. I mean . . . this Johnny Flowers. He's insanely criminal. I mean, he's criminally insane. And his mother! How could you do it? I'm wanted by the police! When they find me it'll be the end. They'll lock me up. I'll never find the Purple Peacock. I won't ever get another job. They'll probably give me twenty years, Nick. Twenty years! That's not to be sneezed at . . .' He pounded his fist into the pillow. Dust rose in a cloud and he sneezed loudly. 'I'll turn myself in,' he went on. 'I'll throw myself on the mercy of the court. Or maybe under a bus. I don't know . . . What am I going to do?'

I waited until he'd quietened down, then I sat next to him.

'Listen,' I said. 'I didn't do it, Herbert. I never stole the carbuncle.'

'But Nick. The judge . . .'

'I was framed, Herbert. I didn't know it at the time – although maybe I should have guessed . . .'

Slowly I explained everything that had happened. The visit from Snape and Boyle, the Fence, Woburn Abbey, Johnny Powers. Then I explained it again using words with fewer syllables. It took me about twenty minutes and all the time he sat there, grasping the mattress. I wasn't sure he'd grasped anything else. But when I finally stopped he stared at me and scratched his head.

'You mean . . . you didn't do it?' he said.

'That's what I've been trying to tell you, Herbert.'

'And the only people who know are Snape and Boyle? But Snape and Boyle . . .'

'Yeah. They bought it.'

'They bought the carbuncle?'

'No. They crashed. They're dead.'

'So what do we do now?'

I stood up and went over to the door. 'I don't know,' I admitted. 'I guess the only thing we can do is try to track down this Fence that everyone wants. If the police ever catch up with us, it might be something to bargain with. But in the meantime . . .' I swung round on Herbert '. . . you've got to convince Johnny and Ma Powers that you're a real crook. If they ever find out you're a private eye, it'll be curtains for us.'

Herbert glanced at the window. 'This place could do with some curtains,' he said.

'They'll kill us, Herbert! I mean really kill us. You've got to think like a gangster. Act like a gangster. Be a gangster. And you've got to start now.'

Herbert got to his feet and straightened his shoulders, drawing his hands across his chest. He gave me an ugly sneer and threw back his head. 'I'm Al Capone,' he growled.

'Al Ka-seltzer more like,' I muttered but I don't think he heard me.

I left him there and went into the bathroom. I meant to have a wash before I turned in. And that was where I had my first big break of the day. I'd turned on the tap and watched it cough out a trickle of brown sludge when I heard a door open underneath me. Quickly I turned it off again. I've mentioned that you could see the bath from the living room through a hole in the ceiling. Well, the same hole allowed me to eavesdrop on a conversation between Ma Powers and her son. And they thought they were alone.

'Your headache gone, Johnny-boy?' she was saying.

'Yeah, Ma. Ya made it better for me.'

'Ya going to be OK when the gang gets here?'

'I'm gonna be just fine.'

'Ya gotta show them who's boss around here, Johnny-boy. With Big Ed trying to move in on ya . . .'

'I got plans for Big Ed, Ma.'

I knelt down and peeped through the hole. From that angle I could just make out the back of Johnny's head. Ma Powers was somewhere out of my vision. That was just as well. If I couldn't see her, she couldn't see me.

'First we're gonna do a raid,' Johnny went on. 'Something really big . . . ya know, to put myself back on the map. Maybe the Bank of England or the Crown Jewels. I don't know. Then I'm gonna go gunning for Big Ed.'

'Ya'll need guns, Johnny.'

'Sure, Ma. That's why I'm gonna see the Fence later today – before the meeting.'

My ears pricked up at that. It seemed almost too good to be true. And what Ma Powers said next was even better.

'So ya're going to Penelope?' she asked.

'That's right. I'll buy enough guns to start a war.'

'Then ya'd better get some sleep, Johnny. I don't want my boy starting no war with bags under his eyes.'

'Ya're good to me, Ma.'

'I love ya, Johnny.'

They went back into the bedroom after that and I heard no more. But as I straightened up and went back into my own bedroom, I was feeling better than I'd felt in a long, long time. Snape and Boyle might be dead. I might be wanted by the police. But at last I knew something about the Fence. He wasn't a man. He was a woman. And the woman's name was Penelope.

10
Vanishing Act

Herbert woke me up six hours later, in time for lunch. I opened my eyes, then shut them again. Taking a deep breath, I opened them for a second time. I groaned. I really was seeing what I thought I was seeing. And I still couldn't believe it.

I'd told Herbert to act like a gangster. He'd taken me at my word and found a costume to match. He had changed into an old-fashioned grey suit, double-breasted with buttons running down both sides, a white shirt and a narrow tie. There was a hat to match, a soft one with a band running all the way round. It was pulled low over his eyes. So low he could barely see. A handkerchief poking out of his top pocket almost completed the picture. All that was missing was a machine-gun in a violin case.

'Wake up, kid,' he drawled out of the corner of his mouth. 'This is Big Herb talking.'

'Herbert . . .' I mumbled. 'Where did you get that suit?'

'I found it in the wardrobe. There are plenty of clothes for you. So let's move. It's time to eat.'

I opened my mouth to call him back but he'd already gone. Hastily I dressed in a fresh shirt but the same trousers and shoes that I'd worn at Strangeday Hall. It was just as well I kept those shoes. I didn't know it then, but they were going to save my life.

But I wasn't thinking of shoes as I went back downstairs. I was wondering what Ma Powers and Johnny were going to make of my brother's performance. They were still in shock when I got in. Ma Powers had cooked up a spaghetti and Johnny and Nails Nathan were each holding a forkful, the white strands coiling down, staring at Herbert.

'OK, Johnny,' Herbert was saying. 'Whassa rap?'

'Herbert . . .' I began. 'I don't think . . .'

That was as far as I got. Herbert reached out and pulled me to him, almost tearing the shirt off my back. 'The name is Big Herb, you dirty rat,' he said. He winked quickly at me and let me go. I sank into a chair, unable to stand.

'Is he OK?' Johnny said.

'Yeah.' I tried to think of something to say. But for once I was lost for words.

'You want some spaghetti?' Nails asked.

'No thanks.' I shook my head. 'I'm not hungry.'

I don't know how I lived through that meal. Nobody spoke and the silence was broken only by the occasional grunt or hiss from Herbert.

Johnny threw down his fork. 'I gotta go out,' he said. He glanced at Herbert. 'Your brother OK, kid?' he asked.

'Sure, Johnny,' I said. 'He's just a bit over-excited.'

'Maybe ya'd better look after him.'

'I'll do that, Johnny.'

He stood up and touched the back of his hand briefly against his mother's cheek. 'Make sure ya get back in time for the meeting, Johnny-boy,' she said.

'That's right, Johnny-boy,' Herbert agreed.

Johnny's eyes were suddenly cold. But he kept himself under control. 'I'll be back in a couple of hours,' he said. 'Nobody leaves the house until I get back. Ya got that?'

He went into the downstairs bedroom to put on a coat. At the same time I grabbed Herbert and dragged him towards the stairs. Ma Powers watched us go. Her eyes were ugly with suspicion – and they hadn't been that great to start with.

Somehow I managed to get Herbert back into our room. I slammed the door shut behind me. 'Are you crazy?' I almost screamed.

'But Nick . . .' Herbert looked at me innocently. 'You said . . .'

'I said act like a gangster. But that doesn't mean . . .' I sighed. There was no point in arguing with him. And I didn't have time.

I went over to the window and opened it.

'What are you doing?' Herbert asked.

'I'm going,' I said. 'Johnny's got an appointment with the Fence and I mean to be there.'

'How do you know?'

'I'll tell you later.' I swung a leg over the window-sill. 'Cover for me until I get back.'

'What shall I tell them?'

'Tell them I've gone back to sleep.'

'But what if they find you gone?'

'I don't know.' I shrugged. 'Tell them I've gone out to get some cigarettes.'

'But Nick . . .' Herbert pleaded. 'You don't smoke.'

'Then tell them it was chocolate cigarettes.'

I pulled myself over the ledge and looked around me, trying to find a way down. That wasn't difficult. The window wasn't that high up to start with and there was a pile of rubble climbing half-way up the wall. I let go and dropped on all fours . . . as quiet as a cat. Actually I landed on a cat. It screeched and howled then shot away in a cacophony of rolling tins and breaking glass. So much for stealth! Johnny Powers would have heard it all on the other side of the river. I crouched for a minute breathing heavily, wondering if anyone would come and look. If they found me there, I'd tell them I'd fallen out of bed. But nobody came. My luck was holding out. It must have been a black cat I'd landed on.

I hurried round the backs of the houses trying not to turn over too many loose bricks with my feet. On the other side I heard a door open and close.

'See ya, Ma.'

'Look after yaself, Johnny-boy.'

As I reached the end of the terrace, Johnny Powers walked into sight making steady progress back towards the river. I ducked back round the corner and waited there, my shoulders pressed against the brick until he passed. I let him get a short way ahead. Then I followed.

He reached Wapping High Street and turned right. I let him turn a corner before I ran forward. This was a Saturday and the road was deserted, the building sites still empty. On the one hand that was good news. With my face on TV and doubtless back in the papers I didn't want to be seen by any passers-by who might try and stop me doing just that. But on the other hand, it made it doubly difficult to follow Powers without being spotted by him. If he turned round there would be no one between us, no crowd for me to melt into. Apart from a few cars parked along the side of the road – as ancient and as dusty as the buildings themselves – there was no cover.

But fortunately he didn't turn round. Johnny's mind was on other things: Big Ed and the Fence to name but two. Also he still trusted me. He had no reason to think he was being followed.

I reached the corner just in time to see Powers walk into a tube station – Wapping Station on the Metropolitan Line. What did I do now? I didn't have any money on me so I couldn't buy a ticket and anyway someone would be sure to see me in the crowded Underground. But that was also true of him. The more I thought about it, the crazier it seemed. Powers was Public Enemy Number One. He couldn't just get on a tube train with a return ticket to the West End.

I didn't think about it long. I'd come this far and I wasn't going to give up now. Maybe he was meeting this Penelope woman on the platform. Maybe there was an exit leading to the river on the other side.

There was a small kiosk on the right but with no one in it. The way down to the platforms was on the other side. I slipped past quickly without being stopped. And now I could hear Johnny Powers, walking ahead of me, his footsteps echoing upwards. A staircase led down into the gloom and there were also two lifts. I thought of taking one of them but that would have meant arriving ahead of him. If he doubled back, I would miss him. I made for the stairs.

A central shaft plummeted downwards with the concrete staircase sweeping round the edge in a great curve. The walls were white, the paint blistered and flaking. The air was cold and dank, carrying with it the smell of the Thames. And yet in the middle the lifts, bright red and modern, soared smoothly up and down. They were time capsules. The rest of the station had got stuck in the turn of the century.

From above, I saw Johnny Powers head off for the southbound platform. So he was planning to travel away from the centre of London – over to Rotherhithe and New Cross! I took the last twenty steps two at a time, afraid now that a train would come and I would miss him. But there was no train. I caught my breath at the bottom of the staircase and then, keeping close to the wall, edged forward towards the platform. Carefully, I peered round.

Johnny Powers had vanished.

I walked on to the platform, two rows of neon tubes casting a hard, frozen light all around me. Beside me, the tunnel to Rotherhithe was black and impenetrable, the glittering rails swallowed up in the darkness after only a few feet. A television screen had been mounted beside the tunnel for the driver. Its flickering picture told me what I had seen the moment I'd arrived. Apart from myself, there was nobody in the station. No passengers, no trains, no guards . . . nothing.

I continued down the platform. A bare brick ceiling curved over the station, open to the sky at the far end. The only sound was the drip of water from above. It was trickling through a confusion of plants and weeds that had somehow found some sort of life to cling on to against the old bricks. A rat scurried along between the rails and disappeared under the platform. There was no sign of Powers. But nor was there another way out. So he had to be here somewhere.

I'd reached the end and was starting back again when there was a soft rumble and a moment later a train burst through the tunnel on my side of the station. I turned round and pretended to read a panel that told you about the history of the place. That way nobody would be able to see my face. Even so, I glanced over my shoulder, waiting for Powers to appear. Two people got off the train and walked towards the exit. Nobody got on. The doors slid shut. There was a hiss and the train moved off again.

There was a drawing of the tunnel on the wall in front of me. The panel told me that it was the oldest tunnel in London, built by Marc Brunel between 1825 and 1843. In those days you'd have walked through or, I suppose, ridden in a horse-drawn carriage. Could you walk through now?

I went back up to the tunnel entrance. I could still hear the train, rumbling away in the distance. But somehow I didn't think Powers was there. It was too dark, too dangerous. One false step, brush against the electric rail, and you'd fry. And there were the trains themselves, hurtling towards you through the darkness. You'd have to be crazy to walk down there. True, Johnny Powers was crazy. But the Fence surely wasn't – and nor was I.

I was about to leave when I noticed a door. A few steps led down from the platform at the very edge of the tunnel. There was a narrow walkway past three fire-buckets and an antique fuse-box. Then a brown door.

It seemed worth a try and there was no one around. I slid past the sign warning passengers not to proceed beyond this point and proceeded beyond it. At first I thought the door was locked. I pushed and I pulled without success. Just when I was about to give up, I realized that it was a sliding door. It slid open. I found a light switch and turned it on.

But the door was another disppointment. It opened into a small room, empty but for two telephones, a few scraps of litter and about fifty years' worth of dust. One side led into a storage area. The other was covered by white tiles with a tap jutting out. If Powers had come in here, he wasn't here now. It led exactly nowhere. I turned the light off. Powers had lost me and I knew it. But I still didn't know how.

There was nothing for it but to go back to the house before I was missed. I took the lift back to street level and hurried out of the station without being seen. Where had Powers gone? He hadn't taken a train and he couldn't have walked through the tunnel. There was nowhere to hide, no way I could have missed him. It seemed unfair. I'd thought he was going to lead me to the Fence. But it had just turned out to be a blind alley.

I kicked at an empty cigarette packet and walked

back down the road with my hands in my pockets. If I hadn't been so disappointed I might have been a bit more alert. I remember that I heard the car coming but didn't think twice about it. When it slowed down, I should have reacted. I turned round when I heard its doors opening – but then it was too late.

Somebody leapt on me from behind. I was pulled off my feet. I shouted out and tried to twist free. Then a fist hit me in the jaw. The strength drained out of me. Helpless, I was bundled into the car. And then we were away.

My mind was reeling. Half my teeth felt like they were about to say goodbye to the other half. I'd thought at first that I'd been caught by the police. But already I knew that it wasn't the police. No. This was something worse.

11
Big Ed

There were three of them in the car. I was in the back seat wedged between two of them. The third drove. There was a nodding dog on the ledge behind me. Only it wasn't nodding any more because somebody had pulled off its head. That was the sort of people they were. The sort of people who could visit the Chamber of Horrors and upstage the exhibits.

The driver was a punk. He had close-cropped, bright green hair and two studs in his ear. There was a tarantula tattooed on the back of his neck. He was chewing gum and every time he moved his mouth it writhed like it was trying to find a way out of his skin. That was all I could see of him from where I was sitting. It was enough to make me wish that I was sitting some place else.

The two other men – they were both in their thirties – could have been brothers. Or sisters. They were somewhere in between. The fat, unshaven cheeks, the enormous biceps, the beer guts and the balding heads . . . that was all definitely masculine. But I wasn't so sure about the handbags and the floral dresses. One of them had a scar running from his eye to his cheekbone. He'd tried to hide it with a dab of powder, but it needed something more. A large paper bag for example.

Nobody said anything for about five minutes by which time we'd crossed the river, heading south west. I shifted in my seat and one of the heavies dug his elbow into my ribs.

'Keep still, pretty-boy,' he said in a voice so deep that it seemed to come from his knees.

'Where are we going?' I asked. 'Who are you guys working for?'

'You'll find out soon enough.'

The punk giggled, making the tarantula dance. I gritted my teeth. This wasn't the first time I'd been 'taken for a ride'. But I was beginning to think that if I didn't make a move soon, it could well be the last. It didn't seem fair. I was too young to die. And to be murdered by two men in women's clothes! What would my parents say?

I made my move when the car slowed down for a red traffic light. I thought I'd timed it perfectly. We were in heavier traffic. One of the thugs was staring out of the window. The other was sitting back with his eyes half-closed. Grab the handle, slam the door open and I'd be out before they knew it. That was the idea.

But I'd under-estimated them. I lurched forward. My hand moved all of six inches. Then one of them grabbed me. I tried to shout out, to get the attention of the other drivers. I hadn't even opened my mouth before something hit me, hard, on the side of the neck. I think it was a handbag. The car span. I thought of the nodding dog. Then I was out.

When I woke up, I was back behind bars – but not exactly in a prison. It was a long narrow building that wasn't quite a building but that was somehow familiar. My head was hurting and there was a nasty taste in my mouth. Otherwise I was more or less OK.

There was a sound outside. A rush and a shudder and a loud clinking. It told me what sort of building I was in. I should have known from the bare planks, the metal grill, the corridor almost as narrow as my prison, the square windows and the communication cord. This was the guard's van of a train. But it was a train that wasn't moving. So where were we then? Victoria Station?

I sat there for about two hours. It had been almost dark when I woke up but now it was darker. I could see the light fading behind the screens that covered the windows. I expected the train to jolt forward at any time, but it never did. I was getting hungry. I hadn't eaten since breakfast and I was beginning to hope that a guard might wander through with a British Rail sandwich when the door opened and the punk appeared in the corridor.

He was still chewing gum and giggling. He had a safety pin in his nose and it wasn't just there for decoration. It was holding the whole thing together. He had the sort of face that looked like it could fall apart at any moment. Chalk white and rotten. Perhaps you've seen those ads that warn you about using drugs. This guy obviously hadn't.

He produced a bundle of keys, unlocked the door and slid it open. I got to my feet. 'If you've come to check my ticket, I haven't got one,' I said.

He giggled.

'Do you speak English?' I asked.

He jerked his head back the way he had come. He didn't speak at all.

I followed him out of the guard's van and across the coupling to the next carriage. The windows were uncovered here and looking out I saw that we were parked in a siding, next to some sort of stock yard. A tall stack of wood obstructed most of the view but I could also see coils of barbed wire and oil drums. The yard was fenced off. There was nobody in sight.

The second carriage was a sleeping carriage. We walked past five doors, the fifth of which was open. Glancing in I saw a two-poster bed. They'd had to cut off the other two posters to fit it in. There was a plush carpet on the floor and an antique chest under the window. A chandelier hung from the ceiling. None of it had been supplied by British Rail. That much I knew for sure. But I wasn't so sure about anything else.

We reached the third carriage. It was blocked off by a plain wooden door that also looked out-of-place on a train. The punk knocked and opened it. We went in.

Classical music. That was the first thing I heard. Bach or Vivaldi played on an expensive stereo system. The whole carriage had been re-vamped by an interior designer with expensive tastes. Silk wallpaper, silk curtains, two more chandeliers . . . the furniture could have come straight out of Woburn Abbey. A cocktail cabinet stood beside the door. One of the walls was lined with books. There was a fireplace at the far end with one of those artificial fires blazing artificially.

The two Beverly sisters from the car were sitting

together on a chaise-longue. One of them was reading a Mills & Boon romance. The other was knitting. There were two other people in the room. One was a woman, wearing a satin dress that was tight in all the right places and tighter still in some of the wrong ones. Her hair was the sort of vivid blonde that can only come out of a bottle. The other was a man. I guessed he was in charge.

He was around fifty, wearing one of those Noel Coward dressing gowns – patterned silk with wide lapels and a cravat. He had a shock of white hair, so white that it did look as if he'd had a shock. His eyes were almost colourless too. He was smoking a cigarette in a long black holder and sipping a Martini cocktail.

'Good evening,' he said. 'I'm Big Ed.'

I shrugged. 'You don't look that big to me,' I said.

One of the sisters looked up from his book. He was the one who'd hit me. 'You don't talk to Big Ed like that,' he grunted.

'Why not?' I asked. I rubbed the back of my neck. 'He gave me a big ed-ache.'

The punk giggled again. Big Ed flicked ash from his cigarette.

'Nicholas Simple,' he said. He had a soft, tired voice that was almost a whisper. 'It's very nice to see you. I have to say that I was dying to meet you.'

'Shame you couldn't do it sooner,' I said.

He ignored me. 'I had my boys out looking for Johnny Powers,' he went on. 'It was his good luck that they missed him. And your bad luck that they found you.' He put down the cigarette and swirled the olive in his glass. 'We'll catch up with him later. But the question now is, what do we do with his number two?'

'How about a drink and a sandwich?' I suggested.

He shook his head. 'Oh no. You see, I had a gun sent in to Strangeday Hall. Three of my boys were going to rub Johnny Powers. It seems you got in the way. One of them was burnt – Zuckie Hommel. Now his own mother doesn't recognize him. And the thing is, you see, she's my sister. Zuckie is my nephew.'

That was bad news. Uncle Ed wasn't smiling any more and there was a flicker of colour in his eyes – a dull red.

'I'd like to know where Powers is,' he said. 'I could ask you. But of course you wouldn't let on.'

'I don't know,' I muttered. 'We could come to some sort of arrangement . . .'

'I don't think so.' His lips curled. 'The only arrangements you should be thinking of are the ones for your funeral.'

He stood up and moved towards me. I thought of attacking him, maybe grabbing an antique lamp and going for his head, but I quickly forgot it. The punk was right behind me. And the two ugly sisters had already shown how fast they could move.

'I'm going to get Johnny Powers,' Big Ed continued. 'South London and East London will be mine. What's the world coming to when you've got kids running the rackets? I don't like kids. I don't like you, Simple. That's why you've got to go.'

He waved a hand at the window.

'This is my hide-out,' he said. 'The police can't

find it. Nobody knows it. But Clapham Junction is only a few minutes away. I bought these carriages and converted them ten years ago. The siding is disused. But we're right next to one of the busiest stretches of railway in England.'

'What's this got to do with me?' I asked.

'I just thought you'd like to know where you're going to die,' he said. 'And how. The railway . . .' He looked at his watch and snapped his fingers. The punk grabbed me from behind. 'Take him out and do it, Spike,' he ordered. 'Scarface and Tootsie – you go with him.' The two drag artists stood up. 'Goodbye, Simple,' he said. 'Remember Zuckie. Remember me. And have a nice death.'

I was dragged out of the carriage. It must have been double-glazed because as soon as I was out in the night air I could hear the trains, clanking and rattling through the darkness. It had begun to rain. At first it was a light drizzle but as I was pulled, kicking and fighting through the stockyard and on to the rails, it came down more heavily. It was a real cloudburst. In seconds the four of us were drenched.

Because of the rain I saw little of my surroundings. I could just make out the lights of Clapham Junction Station blinking in the distance.

We crossed about six or seven rails, our feet crunching on the gravel. Once we stopped as an Intercity Express thundered past, the windows a blur of yellow. I thought someone might see us but in the darkness and the swirling rain that was impossible. Then the punk pushed me between the shoulders. I stumbled and fell. Tootsie and Scarface seized my arms and legs and before I knew what was happening they were tying me down across the rails. The practised way they worked made me think that they must have done it before. It took them less than a minute. But when they straightened up I was fixed as firmly as an oven-ready chicken. My hands were tied to one rail, my legs to the other. My neck rested on the cold metal. My body slumped in between.

Then the gangster called Tootsie squatted down beside me. His hair was all over his face and his make-up was running. But he was smiling.

'Only one more train runs on this track tonight,' he said. 'It comes in around ten minutes. It doesn't stop until it gets to Waterloo. It won't stop for you.'

'Wait a minute . . .' I began, but then he stuffed a handkerchief into my mouth. I tried to spit it out. He twisted another loop of rope around my head, gagging me.

'No one will see you,' he hissed. 'No one will hear you. Ten minutes. Think about it, pretty-boy. In ten minutes you won't be so pretty no more.'

The punk giggled one last time. Tootsie stood up and adjusted his dress. Then, linking arms with Scarface, he walked away. I was left alone, spread out on the track. The rain was falling harder than ever.

12
Off the Rails

One day I'm going to write a book. It will be called 'Sticky Situations' by N. Simple. But don't look for a chapter called 'How to untie yourself from rails in the pouring rain with an Intercity 125 thundering towards you at 90 mph'. You won't find it. Because I tell you now, it can't be done.

As soon as Tootsie, Spike and Scarface had gone, I tried to move my feet, but I could barely wiggle my toes. I tried to slide my hands under the rope. I had about as much chance of flying. They had tied me down tight. The rope was biting into my flesh, cutting off the circulation. The rain didn't help either. It was coming down so hard that it was blinding me, making it impossible to see what I was doing. But I suppose that it didn't matter too much. I was doing precisely nothing. There was nothing I could do.

There was a sudden rumble in the air. I twisted round just in time to see an enormous train come battering through the rain. At least it looked enormous from where I was lying. I tried to call out but the gag stopped me. Now I could see the driver, smoking, high up in the front of the train. My whole body stiffened, waiting for it to ride over me. I think I muttered a prayer. Personally I don't believe in God. The way things had been going recently it looked as if God didn't personally believe in me. But either way, better safe than sorry . . .

The train was almost on top of me. Then there was a loud clattering sound and it jerked away to one side. Someone, somewhere had changed the points. The train continued parallel to me, running along the next track. My head must have been only a couple of feet away from its wheels. That was nasty . . . but it was better than being right under them. I could see all the cables and pipes of its undercarriage. It was a long train.

The rain sliced down. Somewhere a light blinked from red to green. I heard a click as another point was changed and a rail slid across to carry the next train to its correct destination. A solitary pigeon flew in a ragged arc above me. The clouds rolled over.

Suddenly I was trembling. That was strange because I thought I'd been trembling all along. But then I realized that it wasn't just me. It was the rails beneath me. They were vibrating, softly at first but more violently with every second that passed. I couldn't hear anything. I couldn't see anything. But I knew the train was approaching. And this time it was approaching on my track.

I think I went berserk right then. I struggled furiously, my body heaving, my arms and legs tearing at the ropes. But it was useless. All I managed to do was to bruise my ankles and tear my trousers. I forced myself to go limp. Things weren't so bad, I told myself. I mean, there are worse things in life than being run over by a train. I tried to think of one of them. I couldn't. I went berserk again.

I was still heaving and twisting when I heard the blast of the whistle in the distance. It scoured through the night like a red hot poker. The train couldn't have been more than a mile away. That gave me perhaps a couple of minutes of life. Here lies Nick Simple, aged thirteen years, seven months and a couple of minutes. Rest in pieces.

Then the man appeared.

I think it was a man. He had come out of nowhere. He was standing over me, his head about a mile away from his feet. He was wearing an anorak with the hood drawn over his head and in the slanting rain I couldn't make out his face.

'Ngg,' I said. 'Mmn, ngg, nyun . . .'

It wasn't easy making polite conversation with the gag.

He leant down and for a second I thought he was going to plunge the knife into me, to finish me off before the train arrived. But instead the blade cut through the ropes holding my wrists. I sat up, tearing at the gag. The rails were shaking like crazy now. It felt like a long electric shock.

The man dropped the knife and walked away. He hadn't said a word. I had no idea who he was – and yet somewhere in the back of my mind I thought I knew him. Thick-set, wide shoulders. Perhaps a wisp of fair hair showing under the hood. That was all I saw. He had already gone.

'Come back!' I shouted.

He ignored me and I didn't shout again. The last thing I wanted to do was to let Big Ed know I was free, and anyway there was no time for a chat. I could see the train now. The single lamp at the front glowed like a Cyclop's eye. I snatched up the knife and hacked at the ropes holding my ankles. My arms wouldn't obey me. The knife slipped out and I winced as I managed to stab myself in the foot. The train was only yards away now. The bellow of the engine filled my ears. I cut one rope – then the other. The train crashed forward. But I was free. I threw myself off the rails. Another second and it would have been too late.

'Ker-thud, ker-thud, ker-thud, ker-thud . . .'

It might have been the wheels of the train. It might have been the sound of my own heart. But that was all I heard as I lay there, clutching the ground. The train went past, travelling between me and my mysterious rescuer. By the time it had gone and the tracks were clear once again, he had vanished. Who was he? And why hadn't he hung around to let me thank him? Broad shoulders and fair hair. None of Big Ed's men answered to that description. But nobody else could have possibly known I was there.

I stood up and staggered to keep my balance. I wasn't exactly in great shape. I couldn't feel the blood in my fingers. In fact I couldn't even feel my fingers. I'd torn my trousers, gashed my leg. I was soaking wet and bruised all over. But I had to admit, I'd have been in worse shape if I hadn't been cut free. Who had it been? And how had he found me?

I didn't intend standing around in the middle of Clapham Junction working out the answers. That could come later. Right now I had to get away – but even as I moved I realized that my problems were far from over. If I went back to Wapping, I'd have to explain my absence to Johnny and his mother. Worse still, Herbert had been alone with them for the best part of twelve hours. Twelve hours with him and they'd be sure to smell a rat – a dirty rat, it went without saying.

Somehow I had to win their trust back. And the best way to do that was sitting only a hundred yards away in a disused railway siding. I had a score to settle with Big Ed anyway. I was cold, bruised, soaked and exhausted. And I was angry. There was nothing Johnny wouldn't do for me if I took Big Ed out of the picture. I even had an idea how to go about it.

I went back to the siding. The oil-drums. I'd noticed them when they'd taken me out to the rails . . . ten metal barrels with two words stencilled in red on each of them. HIGHLY INFLAMMABLE. Just then the same two words applied to my temper. These weren't nice people. It was high time something horrible happened to them.

There were no lights on behind the windows as I approached Big Ed's carriage. I was afraid he might have posted guards, but there was nobody around. And why should there have been? He had told me himself that the police didn't know where to find him and he certainly wouldn't be expecting a visit from me. He would be sound asleep in his two-poster bed. Spike, Scarface and Tootsie would be slumbering in the next carriage. But not for long . . .

The rain was beginning to slacken off. Fortunately the moon was still hidden behind thick cloud. Careful not to make a sound, I limped away from the carriage and over to the oil-drums. I tapped one with a finger. It was full. Each drum was secured with a metal cap set in the top near the rim. I tried turning one. At first it resisted and I thought it had rusted firm. But by using the knife, cutting into the groove, I was able to free it. I opened four of the cans. The rich smell of kerosene filled my nostrils.

The drums were too heavy to lift. Using all my strength I up-ended one and lowered it as gently as I could. Even so it hit the ground with something between a clang and a crash and it was another couple of minutes before I could find the courage to move. Nothing stirred inside the carriage.

I rolled the first of the drums across the yard until it came to rest against the wheels of the front carriage – the one with the chandeliers and cocktail cabinet. The oil or whatever it was slopped out forming a sticky pool on the ground. I was careful not to get any of it on me but by the time I'd finished I still smelt like a garage on a busy day. I'd opened four cans. I rolled three of them across, one for each carriage. Apart from the crunch of gravel and the gurgle of escaping oil, I made no sound. Five minutes later, a miniature lake had formed around Ed's hide-out. And still the oil spluttered out of the open cans.

Wiping my hands on my trousers – it made them dirtier rather than cleaner – I went back to the fourth can. This one I rolled in the opposite direction, away from the carriages and back on to the rails. Hoisting it up on to the rails themselves was the difficult part. It weighed a ton. But after that it was easy. The rims fitted neatly on to the rails and with no friction it rolled effortlessly. There was a slight gradient down to Clapham Junction Station and I had no trouble with the points. Using only one hand I was able to roll it all the way, leaving a trail of glimmering oil behind me.

By now you should have got the picture. A pool of highly inflammable liquid underneath Big Ed's hide-out. A long trail of the same stuff leading down to the station. 'Light the blue touch-paper and retire quickly' as it says on your average firework. I had fireworks in mind – and Big Ed was about to put in for permanent retirement.

Clapham Junction Station had shut down for the night by the time I got there. When I climbed on to one of the outer platforms I was alone. The fourth drum was almost empty now and I was just about able to heave it up on to the platform and lead the trail of oil past a chocolate vending machine and along to the very door of a telephone kiosk. I left it there while I went to look for a match. That took me longer than I'd thought. Eventually I found a book of matches inside a Waiting Room. There was one left inside.

I went back to the telephone and dialled 999. The operator came on and asked me which service I wanted. I told her police. There was a click, a pause, then a voice.

'This is the police. What number are you calling from?'

'Listen,' I said. 'Are you interested in finding Big Ed?'

My words were met by a long silence. I could imagine the confusion at the other end. There was another click. Perhaps they were trying to trace the call. That didn't bother me. I'd be gone long before they arrived.

'Hello, caller?' another voice asked. Or maybe it was the same voice. I didn't care.

'I know where you can find Big Ed,' I said. 'If you want him.'

'Who is this speaking?'

'Never mind that.' I shivered. It had got colder. 'Do you want him or don't you?'

'We want him.' This was the second voice. They must have transferred the call even as I was speaking. 'Where is he?'

'He has three railway carriages in a siding just outside Clapham Junction Station,' I said. 'Next to the stockyard.'

'There are lots of stockyards around there,' the voice said. 'How do we know which one is his?'

I didn't answer. Propping the telephone under my chin, I struck the match. It glared up in the confined space of the telephone box. With the fumes of the oil all around me I was surprised we didn't blow up then and there. I threw the match on to the platform. The oil caught alight. I watched the flames scurry across the platform, over the edge and on to the rails. Like some sort of mythical animal, with feathers of fire, it sped into the night, heading for Big Ed's carriage.

'How do we find him, caller?' the voice insisted.

'It won't be difficult,' I said. And hung up.

13
World's End

I was more careful when I left Clapham Junction. I was still soaking wet. I stank of oil. I had to cross London with just about the entire population on the look-out for me. And when I got back to Wapping, I'd probably be shot. But otherwise I didn't have anything to worry about. I was having a really lovely day.

I stepped into the shadows as a couple of police-cars raced past, sirens screaming. Perhaps it was seeing them that made up my mind for me. There was no point in going back to Johnny Powers and his gang quite yet. Even if they did lead me to the Fence, there would be little I could do with the information. Because with Snape and Boyle dead, who would believe my story? Even Herbert had taken a lot of convincing and he knew me better than anyone.

But just suppose somebody had seen the two policemen when they visited me at the school. Chief Inspector Snape and his unsmiling assistant weren't the sort of people you could forget in a hurry. If I could prove that they'd been there before the Woburn Abbey incident, the rest of my story might be more credible. The only question was – who might have seen them? It had been late on a Tuesday afternoon when they had come. Everyone else had gone home. That's what they had been waiting for – to catch me there alone.

But there was one person. Noel Harvey St John Palis would have been there. It would have been just like him to stay behind in the staff room to make sure I didn't slip away. And the staff room was directly between the front entrance and my classroom. If anyone had seen the two policemen it would have been him. And by coincidence, I knew where the French teacher lived. I'd been late once with a composition and he'd told me to deliver it to his home – a flat just off the King's Road near the bit known as World's End. I could go there now. It was less far to walk than Wapping. And I'd almost certainly find him in.

I set off, keeping to the shadows. I was more likely to be smelt than to be seen. If anybody stopped me, I'd tell them that I'd been mugged by a meths-drinker and would just have to hope they didn't recognize me. Mind you, I saw my reflection in a shop window and barely recognized myself. I looked like I'd stepped out of a poster for the NSPCC. My hair was all over the place. There were dark circles under my eyes. My clothes were rags and I seemed to have lost about a stone in weight. Big Ed had a lot to answer for. But on the other hand, by now Big Ed probably looked a whole lot worse.

I followed the 49 bus route back up to the Thames and over Battersea Bridge. The rain had stopped at last – not that that mattered to me any more. Crossing the river was the worst part. Here everything was open and brightly lit. There were a surprising number of cars about, considering how late it was. Each time one passed me I shivered and tried to hide my face. If a police-car had chosen that moment to cross the bridge you could have kissed goodbye to Chapter Fourteen.

In fact I made it as far as Chelsea before I was spotted.

I'd reached the traffic lights on the King's Road and stopped to get my bearings. There were two policemen standing on the other side of the road, outside a National Westminster bank. At first they didn't let on they'd seen me. After all, as far as they knew I was armed and dangerous. Out of the corner of my eye I saw one nudge the other and then talk into the edge of his jacket. He wasn't having a conversation with his armpit. There would be a radio there. He was calling for help.

Casually, I turned left and began to walk down the King's Road to World's End. I didn't need to look back to know that the two policemen were following me. But I still kept up the pretence. I was just an ordinary, innocent boy out for a night walk. The rags and the smell of oil? Nothing to concern you, officer. I always dress this way. I turned a corner and for a moment I was out of their sight. I began to run.

It was already too late. I'd seen it the moment I'd set off – a police-car, heading towards me at seventy miles an hour. And it had seen me too. Suddenly the sirens and blue lights were on and it was swerving across the road to cut me off. With a spurt of energy, I took a sharp left, past a pub and down a narrow street. I heard the screech of wheels as the police-car followed me. The first on the right was

Ann Lane – the road where Palis lived. There was a skip parked outside a development of new flats. I didn't look to see what was inside it. I just dived in head-first.

The police-car tore round the corner and continued down Ann Lane, its siren probably waking up half the residents if not most of Chelsea. As soon as it had gone, I poked my head up. As well as the usual junk, someone had dumped the remains of about a dozen meals in the skip. I hadn't been exactly great to begin with, but now I looked and smelt like a walking compost heap. But I didn't have time to worry about my appearance. Ann Lane was a cul-de-sac and the police-car would be back at any moment. Right now it was my disappearance that mattered more.

I'd taken about ten steps before the sweep of the headlight told me that I could go no further. The police car was on its way back, more slowly now, searching for me. I looked left and right. There was nowhere to hide beside the road, nowhere they wouldn't find me. But what about above the road? There was a car parked awkwardly across the pavement. Without breaking my stride, I ran across the bonnet, on to the roof and then up on to the slanting roof of a garage or lock-up. I'd left some pretty expensive foot-prints behind me on the panel-work, but with a bit of luck nobody would see them. I threw myself flat. The police car stopped.

Just because Palis lived in Chelsea, it didn't mean he was rich. He had a council flat in a long block that looked out over the King's Road in the front and Ann Lane at the back. The flats were all identical, two floors high with net curtains and hanging bowls of flowers and smoked glass windows for the bathrooms which were all in exactly the same place above the front doors. Step out of the door and you would find yourself in a little square garden. All the gardens were cluttered up with prams and bags of old tools. The flats were too small to contain them.

The block was built above a row of shops. The roof I was spread out on now covered the back of one of these shops. Above me there was a white railing. If I climbed over that I'd find myself on the same level as the front doors. In other words, the flats were above me. The police car was below me. I was caught in the middle.

There were footsteps running along the pavment. Looking down I could just make out the helmets of the two policemen who had seen me in the first place. They stopped beside the car.

'Any sign of him?'

'No. He must have doubled back.'

'You sure it was him?'

'No doubt about it. A right little villain . . .'

Well I wasn't going to argue with that provided they went away and left me alone. But then the worst thing possible happened. A light went on overhead. It slanted down, capturing me in a bright square. A door opened and somebody strutted out, leaning over the balcony to call down to the policemen.

'What's going on?' a voice demanded. It was a voice that I knew well.

I twisted round. Palis had come out on to the

balcony, wearing a blue dressing-gown and pyjamas. He was leaning over, looking down at the policemen. From where he was standing, I was directly in his line of vision. He saw me. He couldn't miss me. For a moment he frowned and I froze. One word from him and it would all be over. Desperately I raised a finger to my lips and stared at him with pleading eyes.

'We're looking for someone,' one of the policemen said. 'A young boy . . .'

'Well do you have to make such an infernal racket about it?' Palis asked and I breathed again. For the moment I was safe.

'He's dangerous, sir,' the policeman said.

'And so am I when I'm woken up in the middle of the night,' Palis snapped. 'He obviously isn't here so I suggest you go and wake up somebody else looking for him.'

There was a bit more muffled chat below but then the police car moved away and the two policemen passed underneath the building and back into the King's Road. Palis glanced at me. 'Simple?' he demanded in a tone of disbelief.

'Yes, sir.' I stood up. 'Thank you very much, Mr Palis – sir.'

'You'd better climb up here before anyone sees you,' he said.

I climbed over the rail and joined him on the terrace. 'Thank you,' I said. 'For not turning me in . . .'

He smiled. 'Well, I had a good reason . . .'

'I'm innocent,' I blurted out. 'I didn't do any of

it. In fact I was working for the police from the very start. I still am. Only . . . it's difficult to explain.'

'You'd better come in,' he said.

I followed him into the flat.

It was exactly the sort of place you'd expect a French teacher to live, right down to the model of the Eiffel Tower on the mantelpiece. There was a table piled high with books – French classics, art books and exercise pads from school. There was even a notice-board just like the one outside the staff room, displaying the same sort of information – local theatre programmes, lesson time-tables . . . that sort of thing. Palis was neat and organized but he wasn't rich. The carpet was nylon. The furniture looked second-hand. He lived alone. Somehow I knew without asking.

'Sit down,' Palis said. 'I'll make you some tea.'

'Thank you, Mr Palis.' I sat down beside the table. 'And thanks again for not telling the police. Why didn't you?' I remembered what he'd said out on the terrace. 'You said there was a reason . . .'

'*Exactement*.' Palis nodded. 'I never believed that you were really responsible for the theft of the carbuncle, Simple. Your French is poor. You are often inattentive. But despite all the evidence, I found it hard to believe that you could have allowed yourself to commit such a terrible crime.'

He went into the kitchen. While he prepared the tea, I thumbed through the exercise pads. The bright red lines and the sarcastic remarks in the margin reminded me more of the Palis I knew. This Palis was somehow different. But then put any teacher in a blue dressing-gown and fluffy slippers and you'll find he isn't quite the same.

He came back in carrying two mugs with a plate of biscuits balanced on the top. There was an unpleasant smell in the living-room now. Unfortunately, it was me. Palis pretended not to notice. It was funny. In the last few weeks I'd been framed and sent to prison. I'd escaped, got involved in a mad chase across London, been kidnapped and tied down to a railway track. But sitting here drinking tea with my French teacher in the middle of the night seemed more unreal than any of it.

'So tell me your story, Simple,' Palis said. 'You say you're working for the police . . .'

'Yes, sir – Mr Palis,' I replied. 'That's why I came to see you. Do you remember the time you made me write out all the tenses of "*rire*" when I was mucking around in class?'

'Yes.' He frowned. 'I don't think you've handed them in yet, Simple.'

'I'll do them tonight, sir.'

'No, no. They can wait. Go on . . .'

'Well, that was when they came. I wondered if you saw them. It was a Tuesday afternoon. Two men . . . Snape and Boyle. Big and ugly.'

He shook his head. 'I left the school early that day,' he said. 'I went to the library with "The Hunch-back of Notre Dame".'

'Could he have seen them?'

'I mean the book.'

'Oh.'

So that was that. Palis hadn't seen anything. But once I'd started I had to go on. In answer to his questions I told him everything that had happened to me since then. He didn't interrupt. I couldn't tell whether he believed me or not. By the time I finished, my tea was stone-cold. I hadn't had a chance to drink it.

'This Penelope . . .' he muttered. 'You were sent to find her?'

'Yes.'

'Well, if you can do that maybe your troubles will be over.'

'If anyone believes me,' I said gloomily.

He straightened up. 'I believe you, Simple,' he said. 'I don't know why. It is *un vrai conte*.'

'An old count?' I asked.

'No. An extraordinary story. But I do believe you. The question is – what can I do to help you?'

There was no real answer to that. If Palis hadn't seen Snape then coming here tonight had been a complete waste of time.

'I'll go,' I said.

'In the morning.' He got to his feet. 'Right now you need a hot bath and somewhere to sleep. I have a spare room. Tomorrow I can drive you to Wapping. It seems to me that the sooner you rejoin your brother and this . . . Powers, the better.'

'It may be too late already.'

'Do you have any choice, *mon ami?*'

I spent the rest of the night in a spare room the size of a cupboard. It was almost like being back in my cell except that the door wasn't locked. I fell asleep clutching the pillow. And I dreamt. I dreamt of Herbert in his gangster outfit. I dreamt of Johnny Powers and a lion and an Intercity 125 Express. I thought I heard the tinkle of a bell and somebody talking in a low voice but then the voice became that of the judge sentencing me and I found myself strapped down and realized that I was in the electric chair and Ma Powers was about to throw the switch. I saw her hand move. There was a flash of light and I opened my eyes. The sun was shining through the window, dazzling me. I was awake. And I'd managed to tear the pillow in half.

14
Doorway to Hell

After breakfast, Palis drove me back to Wapping. He was nervous of being seen with me, which was understandable. If he'd been found with me, the only school he'd have ever taught in again would have been a reform school. He made me crouch down in the back seat of his battered Peugeot and didn't speak for the entire journey as if he were travelling alone. I had to admit that I'd misjudged him. He could have called the police at any time during the night and put himself in the clear. He hadn't – and he'd even gone out to buy me a new outfit from a local market near his flat. But I was still wearing my prison shoes.

It was Sunday and Wapping was even emptier than the day before. The rain hadn't left it any prettier either. With no gutters, the roads had nowhere to put the water. It was lying there in wide pools, dirty mirrors reflecting a dirty sky. Palis stopped near the tube station and I got out.

'Thanks, Mr Palis . . .' I began.

'Good luck, Simple,' he said. He was in a hurry to get away, to get back to his safe world of nylon carpets and French composition. 'I hope it all works out. If you need help, get in touch.'

'I will.'

He drove off. His back wheel smashed one of the mirrors, spraying my nice new clothes with mud and water. I took a deep breath. There was nobody around. Now all I had to do was to face up to Johnny Powers and persuade him that I was still on his side.

The real worry was Herbert. He'd been alone with Powers for almost twenty-four hours. I'd have been worried if it had been twenty-four minutes. They'd have asked him questions. Would he have come up with the right answers? One word out of place and he could reserve a place in the nearest cemetery. But Palis had been right. I had no choice. If I didn't go back, Herbert wouldn't stand a chance.

I walked down Wapping High Street to the turn-off where the hide-out stood – or rather leaned against its scaffolding. It all seemed quiet enough. Even so I was aware of a sort of tingling. Call it an alarm bell if you like. Something was wrong but I didn't know what it was. Maybe it was too quiet. Maybe it was something else – something I'd seen or heard.

I stopped beside the front door. I lifted my finger to ring the bell, then thought better of it. Powers wasn't expecting visitors. It would be just like him to put a dozen bullets through the door before he opened it. I went back to the window and peered through. The curtains were drawn. Were they still in bed? It was almost eleven o'clock. But even if they'd all decided to sleep in, they'd have left Nails Nathan on guard. I thought for a minute. Maybe I was being over-cautious. It was quiet in Wapping because it was always quiet in Wapping. There was no one there to make any noise. I'd go in and be welcomed back into the fold. If they were really angry with me, I might get folded a bit before the welcome. But I could handle that. And I did have good news to tell them about Big Ed and his gang.

I went back to the door and reached out again for the bell. And that was when I saw it.

It was the colour that saved me. Wapping was all grey – with the occasional patches of dark brown and black. After a while, your eyes get used to it. You didn't expect to see any colour. But this was bright yellow. It was a piece of plastic, about a quarter of an inch long. It was lying on the door-step. I knelt down and picked it up. There were a couple of copper strands inside. It was a piece of electrical wiring. What was it doing there?

I looked back at the door-bell and suddenly I didn't like it at all. Because suddenly I remembered that when we'd arrived at the hide-out there hadn't been a door-bell. It was brand new. It had been put there specially for me.

Right then I wanted to turn round and go back to the tube station. I could go to the very end of the Metropolitan line and sit there quietly until it was all over. But there was still a chance that Herbert was inside. I made up my mind.

I followed the houses round to the back and went in the way I'd come out – up the pile of rubble and in through my bedroom window. It was harder going up than it had been jumping down. I could only just reach the window sill and when I finally managed to pull myself up, the window was locked. I used my elbow to break the glass. If Johnny and his mother were asleep, I'd wake them up for sure. But I didn't think they were there. I didn't think they'd been there for quite some time.

A quarter of an inch of yellow wire . . .

I hurried through the bedroom noticing that Herbert's bed had been slept in. Nothing else seemed to have been disturbed. Nobody stirred as I moved out on to the corridor, but walking down the stairs I heard a sort of muffled crying. I reached the bottom and stopped dead. I think about two minutes passed before I even dared move.

Herbert was sitting in a chair, tied up and gagged. He was still dressed in a pair of pyjamas but – perhaps as a joke – someone had put the gangster hat back on his head. He was staring at an object on a table only a few feet away from him. It was a Walt Disney alarm clock with Mickey Mouse pointing at the time with his white-gloved hands: seven minutes to eleven. But I didn't think Walt Disney had been resposible for the rest of it. There were six sticks of dynamite attached to the clock. A yellow wire trailed away, leading to the door.

A time bomb. It was set for eleven o'clock. Ring the door-bell and it would have gone off sooner. Herbert, myself and Mickey Mouse would have been blown to smithereens.

I forced myself to move. Herbert had seen me out of the corner of his eye and he was rocking back and forth and grunting. I took the gag off.

'Hello, Herbert,' I said.

'Nick!' he screamed. 'Get me out of here! Help! Do something! Call the police! Call the bomb squad! Where have you been? How could you do this to me?'

For a moment I was tempted to gag him again. I had to move quickly and having him yelling at me wouldn't help. There was no time to untie him. Powers had used wire and it wouldn't cut. The clock showed six minutes to eleven. In six minutes I might just manage to free his legs but Herbert was such a jibbering wreck that I doubted he'd be able to use them.

'This is all your fault,' he went on. 'I should never have helped you escape. It's not fair. What did I ever do to hurt anyone? I should have listened to Mum . . .'

'Herbert,' I said. 'If you don't shut up, I'll leave you here.'

His mouth fell open. 'You wouldn't!'

'Don't tempt me.'

I went over to the table and examined the bomb. It was more complicated than I'd first thought. Apart from the yellow wire there were two coils – red and blue – leading from the dynamite to the clock via a sort of black plastic junction box. The box was closed by a single screw. There was a glass cylinder next to it, a bit like a valve. The whole thing was tied together by two strips of plastic tape.

'What are you going to do?' Herbert whimpered.

'I'm going to defuse it,' I said.

'I don't believe you.'

I shook my head. 'Nor do I . . .'

He fell silent again. I reached out and touched the dynamite. My hand was trembling so hard my fingers were just a blur. It didn't go off. Five minutes to eleven. I tried to think what I knew about bomb disposal. Unfortunately it wasn't one of the subjects they taught at school. But I'd seen films and read books. At eleven o'clock the alarm bell would ring. An electrical contact would be made. The detonator – that was presumably the glass valve – would be activated. It would be the last thing I would see.

Ringing the door-bell would have done the same thing, only earlier. How else could I set the bomb off? It could have a touch sensor of some sort, but I'd already touched it and it hadn't sensed anything. I could cut one of the wires. But I didn't know which one and anyway it was too dangerous. I could move the hands of the clock back. That seemed the most obvious thing to do. In fact it was so obvious it was probably lethal.

My eyes were drawn to the junction box with its single screw. That had to be the answer. Break the electrical circuit and the whole thing would be neutralized. I'd left my knife at World's End. I needed a screwdriver or something with a narrow blade. I straightened up.

'Where are you going?' Herbert demanded.

'Into the kitchen,' I said.

'The kitchen?' Herbert jerked round. 'Nick – this is no time for a cup of tea!'

I ignored him. A minute later I was back with a vegetable knife. It wasn't perfect but at least the blade was flat at the top. Another minute. There were only four left.

My hand was still shaking. I paused for a few seconds and fought to control myself.

Three minutes to eleven.

I leant down and inserted the tip of the knife into the hole at the top of the black box. It slipped and the blade brushed against one of the wires. My heart did a double backward somersault and dived into my stomach. I was sweating now. I could feel it trickling down the sides of my face. Using all my concentration, I pushed the knife back into the right place. It came into contact with the screw. I turned it.

The screw wouldn't move. I tried again, harder. This time I felt the screw give. But would there be another fail-safe device? Would turning the screw be enough to set the whole thing off? It was too late to stop. The knife made three complete revolutions. The screw rose up then fell out. It landed on the table with a little rattle. Herbert squeaked.

I put the knife down and reached for the lid of the box with my finger and thumb. They had never felt bigger or more clumsy. I didn't know how much time had passed. I didn't dare look at the clock. Somehow I got a grip on the plastic and pulled as gently as I could, looking for a wire or a spring mechanism that might join it together. There was nothing. I dropped the lid and wiped the sweat out of my eyes. So far so good.

I had been right about the electrical circuit. Inside the junction box there was a wire and an ordinary switch. It had three positions. At the moment it was in the middle. I could push it to either side. But which side? Make the wrong choice and I wouldn't be given another. I glanced at the clock. I had less than a minute to decide.

'Left or right, Herbert?' I called out.

'Left or right what?' he asked.

'Just say – left or right.'

'Left.'
'Left?'
'Right.'
'Right?'
'No. I mean . . . left's got to be right. Left!'

I pushed the switch to the right. The alarm bell rang. Herbert screamed. But the clock just went on ticking. Mickey Mouse grinned at me. I felt all the strength drain out of me. I'd done it.

It took me half an hour to untie Herbert. My hands were still shaking at the end of it. At last he stood up, took one last look at the bomb and went off to get dressed. I sank limply into his chair. I'd done it. I still couldn't believe it. Upstairs I could hear Herbert thumping about in the bedroom. I sighed. He could at least have remembered to say thanks.

15
Penelope

Ma Powers had left a bit of food in the kitchen and Herbert cooked lunch. He burnt the toast and his eggs weren't so much scrambled as cemented, but I was hungry enough to eat anything. It's funny how extreme danger can give you a big appetite. I'd had two close calls in less than twenty-four hours and it seemed like my stomach was celebrating. I'd drunk three cups of coffee and eaten half a pack of biscuits before I knew what I was doing. If I stayed in this game much longer I was going to get fat. Or dead.

I told Herbert what had happened since I'd left – my encounter with Big Ed and my night with Mr Palis. We thought of ringing the teacher again but there didn't seem much point.

'So who was it, then?' Herbert asked.

'Who?'

'The person who cut you free from the railway.'

I shrugged. 'I've no idea. At least, I thought I'd seen him somewhere before but . . . in the rain, it was impossible to tell.' I cast my mind back to the night before. 'I don't even know how he found me – if it was a he. I was in the middle of nowhere. Nobody knew I was there. It doesn't make sense . . .'

There was less to puzzle about in Herbert's side of the story. In fact I could more or less guess what had happened to him without asking. Left alone with Johnny Powers and with me mysteriously gone, he would have been lucky if he'd lasted ten minutes.

And that was about it. Johnny had got back from wherever he'd been to find me missing. He'd questioned Herbert and he hadn't liked the answers. Suspicion is a fast-growing seed and with Herbert around it had had plenty of fertilizer. He hadn't been invited to the big gangster meeting in the afternoon. The atmosphere during dinner had been as frozen as the fish-fingers Nails Nathan had served. Herbert had gone to bed early only to be dragged out at dawn. Johnny had decided not to take any chances. Herbert had been tied up and gagged . . . and the rest I knew.

'Did he say anything?' I asked.

'He didn't say anything nice,' Herbert muttered.

'I'm sure,' I sighed. 'But did he say anything that might tell us where he is now?'

Herbert thought for a moment. 'He told a sort of joke just as he left,' he said 'That guy Needles Nathan had fixed up the bomb and he said it would blow us both sky high. Then Powers said that was OK because by the time you got back, they'd have gone underground.'

'Underground? Was there anything else?'

'Yes. That was when he put the hat on me. He said something about going to the bank. But he hoped that when the bomb went off, they'd be able to hear it.' Herbert shook his head. 'I think Johnny Powers is just a little bit sick,' he concluded.

That was like calling Hitler a little bit bad. But Herbert had told me what I wanted to know. If Powers hoped to hear the explosion, that had to mean he was somewhere near. 'Going underground' could mean he was simply hiding – or it could mean something more. As for the bank, that didn't make any sense at all. For one thing there were no banks in the area and anyway this was Sunday. They would all be closed.

I hadn't said anything, but Herbert must have read my thoughts because he suddenly sat bolt upright in his chair.

'You're not going to look for him?' he groaned.

'What other choice do we have?' I asked.

'How about going home and forgetting all about it?'

'The police are still looking for us,' I reminded him.

'For you,' Herbert said.

'For *us*. You helped me escape, remember?'

And so we left. Herbert had changed into more ordinary clothes and I was still wearing the gear that Palis had bought. As ever there was nobody around in Wapping, but if anyone happened to pass, they probably wouldn't give us a second glance. I'd found a small back-pack in the cupboard upstairs and I took that too – to make me look more ordinary, I told Herbert.

But that wasn't quite true. I'd defused the bomb and while the switch in the junction box remained on the right, I was fairly sure that it was harmless. So I took it with me in the back-pack. Who could say? It might come in useful.

We spent the rest of the day going round in circles. The light was failing before I realized that we were too. We hadn't found anything. There were a hundred and one places Powers could have chosen to hide out in . . . empty apartment blocks, building sites, half-constructed houses and even derelict mobile homes.

'If only Snape hadn't got killed,' I muttered.

We'd paused for breath, sitting on a low wall beside Wapping High Street. My prison shoes were still pinching and I'd walked enough for one day.

'I thought you didn't like him,' Herbert said.

'I didn't. But right now he's the one person we could go to. He knew the truth. He might be able to help us.'

We didn't speak for a while. Then Herbert frowned. 'Are you sure there aren't any banks around here?' he asked.

'Banks?'

'I'm sure that's what Powers said. He was going to the bank.'

'But the banks are closed.'

'So? He could still rob one.'

Banks. Banks . . .

Suddenly it hit me. I felt so stupid I could have hit myself. We were sitting only half a minute away from the biggest bank in London and I hadn't even thought of it. I got to my feet and threw my backpack across my shoulders, forgetting for a moment what was inside. It would have been just my luck to blow myself to pieces just as I was getting somewhere.

'Where are we going?' Herbert asked.

'To the bank,' I said.

I retraced the steps we'd taken the morning we'd

arrived, back between two warehouses and out on to the jetty. I stopped at the end and looked round. As I remembered, it gave me a good view of the edge of Wapping. Herbert caught up with me and stopped, scratching his head.

'What are you doing?' he demanded.

'The bank, Herbert,' I said. I pointed. 'The river bank. That's what Powers was talking about. He's got to be somewhere here. Right now we're probably looking at him.'

But what were we looking at? First there were the warehouses – King Henry's Wharf on the one side, St John's on the other. Cranes perched on the vertical walls like gigantic grasshoppers, feeding on the brickwork. Further away were the new flats and more jetties with the silver-grey water lapping at their legs. And there was the abandoned houseboat, moored to the quay. There was still something strange about it. I'd noticed it the first time I'd seen it but now I couldn't remember what it was. I looked more closely. There was something wrong, but suddenly it didn't matter any more.

The sun was low and it was hard to see but I could still make out the single word painted on the side of the boat. I might have seen it before if I'd been looking for it. Like all houseboats it had a name. And the name of this one was *Penelope*.

'That's it!' I said. 'Penelope!'

Herbert had seen it too. 'So when Powers said he was going to Penelope . . .' he began.

'. . . he was talking about the houseboat. That must have been where his meeting with the Fence was.'

'But you said he went into the station.'

'He did.' I thought back. 'He must have realized he was being followed. So he used the station to lose me.'

'So what do we do now?' Herbert asked.

'Now? We have a closer look at that boat.'

But that was easier said than done. We followed the road round again only to find that the quay was blocked off by a tall gate with barbed wire at the top. There was no way we could climb over it and no way round the side. That only left one alternative. Fortunately the day had been warm.

'You've got to be joking!' Herbert exclaimed when I told him.

'You don't have to come,' I muttered, unbuttoning my shirt.

'There's got to be another way . . .'

'Can you think of one?'

Herbert thought. Then he unbuckled his belt.

'You're coming with me?' I asked.

'Somebody's got to look after you,' he said.

We left our clothes and the back-pack at the end of the jetty and, wearing only underpants, slipped into the river. It had been a warm day, only the Thames hadn't noticed. The water was freezing. By the time I'd got in as far as my knees I couldn't feel my toes.

The current was strong and it was moving against us. Herbert followed me, doing a dog-paddle that would have disgraced a dog. As well as being around zero degrees centigrade, the water was also filthy. A lot of nasty things floated past on a level with my nose. I tried to swim faster, but every three strokes

I took I was pulled back two. Fortunately it wasn't too far to the boat. But it was still a good five minutes before I pulled myself out.

And that wasn't easy either. The deck of the *Penelope* was a long way above the water and although I pulled on the side of the boat, it refused to tilt. In the end, Herbert had to help me up, pushing from underneath and disappearing under the surface himself at the same time. Then I was lying on the deck, reaching out for him while he coughed and spluttered with a dead fish caught behind his ear. Somehow I pulled him out.

I don't quite know what I was expecting to find on board. I certainly wasn't going to catch Johnny Powers there. In fact the only thing I was likely to catch was pneumonia. And once we'd got inside it looked as if the whole thing had just been one big waste of time.

The boat was empty. There was one big cabin contained in a sort of wooden box with narrow windows and a wide doorway leading on to the deck. The wheel and the engine controls would have been mounted outside, but they'd long gone. The Penelope was a rusting hulk, nothing more. A single room about the size of a coach, floating on the Thames with nowhere to go.

Herbert was standing in the corner, shivering. The fish stared at him, hanging down beside his face.

'Why do I ever listen to you?' he began, stammering on every word as his teeth beat out a flamenco rhythm.

'Wait a minute . . .' I cut in.

It wasn't much to go on. It certainly wasn't worth the swim. But now I reached down and picked it up. It was a small square of paper, white and folded in the middle.

'What is it?' Herbert asked.

'It's a small square paper, white and folded in the middle,' I said. 'A cigarette paper.' I'd recognized it at once. I'd seen Powers rolling them all day long every day I'd known him. 'Powers was here,' I added.

'Well he isn't here now.'

'No. But maybe he'll come back.'

'Nick . . .'

'All right,' I said. 'Let's move.'

Together we made our way back on to the deck. And I was still vaguely aware that there was something wrong. The Penelope wasn't behaving like a boat should. I didn't know what it was, but there was something fishy about it. And I wasn't just talking about the one behind Herbert's ear.

Midnight in Wapping. Herbert and I were crouching in the half-shell of a house directly opposite the gate that led to the quay where *Penelope* was moored. We'd been there roughly six hours. And six hours had never been rougher. We hadn't been able to dry before we got dressed and our clothes were damp and itchy. We were frozen and exhausted. Nobody had so much as driven past for an hour and then it had only been a taxi on its way home. It was a pitch black, moonless night. Even the stars hadn't bothered to show up. The only light came from a street lamp a few yards away, a dull glow that reflected in the windows of the empty ship.

So what were we doing there, watching a deserted quay on a deserted river in a deserted part of town? I couldn't really answer that question myself. It was just that somewhere inside me I was sure that the quay was the key. I was determined to stick with it. Powers had been there once. He might come back. And the Fence might come with him.

'Nick . . . ?' Herbert asked drowsily. I thought he had fallen asleep.

'Yes?'

'Was Strangeday Hall really that bad?'

'It was worse.'

'But was it worse than this?'

I had to admit he had a point. Turn ourselves in and at least we would get a nice cosy cell, fresh clothes and something to eat. The only trouble was, I'd be a teenager when I went in, and an old-age pensioner when I came out.

'Perhaps . . .'

I was about to say something when it happened. It was so totally unexpected that for a moment I thought I must be imagining things. But Herbert had seen it too. His hand gripped my arm. A light had gone on. Inside the empty boat.

A moment later, a figure appeared, climbing over the deck. He had opened the cabin door from inside and was walking down towards us, towards the gate.

'Where did he come from?' I whispered.

'He must have swum,' Herbert said.

'But he isn't even wet.'

'Another boat, then?'

'Did you hear anything?'

Herbert shook his head. Meanwhile the figure had reached the gate and was opening it, turning the padlock with a heavy brass key. He was dressed in dark trousers and shirt. He looked up and down the road, checking that there was nobody in sight. Then he went back to the boat.

'It's impossible . . .' Herbert hissed.

'Sssh!'

There was a soft rumbling and a lorry appeared, its tyres crunching on the gravel. For a moment I thought it was going to drive right past, but then it stopped and reversed, coming to a halt with its back only a yard or so from the gate. It was the sort of lorry you see outside houses when people are moving. The back folded up like a Venetian blind. Two men got out and moved towards *Penelope*.

The first man – the one in the dark clothes – had been joined by three more, each of them carrying a crate the size of a tea-chest. They were walking out of the boat as if they had been there all evening. But I knew that wasn't the case. The boat had been empty when we explored it. It had never been out of our sight since. So where had the men come from – and for that matter, the crates?

And that was only the start. The five men must have made a dozen journeys to *Penelope* and each time they returned to the lorry they were carrying something more. First there were some more crates. Then there was a rack of coats, a stereo system, another dozen crates and finally two oil paintings, each of them bigger than the cabin they'd just come out of.

By now they'd managed to fill an entire lorry from an empty boat. The two men got back inside and it drove off – only to be replaced by a second. Then the whole procedure began again. This time they carried three antique tables, six crates, two rolls of carpet, four life-sized statues and – to cap it all – a grand piano. The piano had to wait for a third lorry to arrive. The way things were going, I wouldn't have been surprised if a ninety-piece orchestra had followed.

'It's impossible,' Herbert muttered for a second time.

And I had to admit, he was right. It *was* impossible. You must have seen that trick magicians do on the stage. They show you an empty hat and then they pull out a rabbit. Well, imagine the same thing only with an elephant and you'll get the general idea.

The whole operation took about half an hour. At last the third lorry moved away. The man in the dark clothes locked the gate and went back to the boat. The light went out and then everything was just as it had been before it started.

For a long time neither of us spoke. Then Herbert broke the silence. 'Nick,' he said, 'do you think you could have missed all that when you searched the boat?'

'Missed it?' I almost screamed. 'You were there too. The boat was empty. We'd have had to be blind to miss it. I mean . . . where do you think it all was? Under the cigarette paper?'

I closed my eyes, trying to work it all out. *Penelope* . . . I'd realized there was something screwy about it from the very start. And now I remembered what it was. It hadn't rocked. The morning we'd arrived in Wapping, I'd seen it. The Thames water chopping and swelling but the boat standing fast. Like it wasn't actually floating.

And then I thought about Johnny Powers. I'd followed him when he'd 'gone to *Penelope*'. I knew what he'd meant by that now. But he hadn't gone anywhere near the quay. So maybe . . .

'Let's move,' I said.

'Where?'

I smiled at Herbert. 'Where do you think? To Wapping Tube Station.'

16
Underground

The tube system had shut down for the night but just for once luck was on our side. The station must have been being cleaned as the door was open and the lights were on. Not that they were expecting anyone to break in. What was there to steal after all? A ticket machine?

Even so, we crept in as quietly as we could – in case there was someone around to stop us. At the last minute I managed to stop Herbert from trying to buy a ticket and we headed for the stairs. Then it was back down the winding staircase and on to the platform where I had lost Powers the first time. The station was as silent as a tomb. The arched brickwork could have come straight out of a cemetery. All it needed was a sixty-foot-long coffin to complete the picture.

We walked to the end of the platform and gazed into the endless night of the tunnel. There would be no tubes for at least five hours. I assumed that meant there would be no electricity in the tracks either. If I was wrong, I might be in for a nasty shock in more ways than one. But I had to be right. The tunnel stretched underneath the Thames. Somewhere there had to be another passageway leading to . . .

. . . but I still had no idea what I'd find at the other end.

'Nick,' Herbert whispered. 'I don't think there's going to be another tube tonight.'

'Herbert!' I thought I'd explained it to him already. 'We're not taking a tube.'

'Well if you're hoping for a bus . . .'

'We're walking!'

'Down there?' Herbert stared at me, his mouth as wide as the tunnel's.

'It'll be easy.'

That was when the lights went out. The darkness hit us, a right hook between the eyes. There must have been somebody in the station after all because a moment later I heard the clatter of the iron gate being drawn across the entrance. Then there was nothing. No sound. No light. You had to pinch yourself to be sure you were still alive.

'Easy?' Herbert's voice quavered out of the darkness.

'Hang on a moment . . .'

Fortunately I still knew what direction I was facing. In the total blackness I could have taken three steps and hurled myself off the edge of the platform. I reached out and found the wall. Then slowly I shuffled towards the tunnel. There were three steps leading down – I remembered them from my first visit. My foot found the top one and I lowered myself down. My shoulder hit one of the fire buckets with a dull clang.

'Who is it?' Herbert squeaked.

'It's only me,' I said.

'Where are you going?'

'To Buckingham Palace,' I growled.

There was a pause. Then – 'Are you sure that's the right way?'

I ignored him. Somehow I found the sliding door. With a sigh of relief I felt it open. I ran my hand up and down the wall, searching for the light switch. I hit it with my thumb. The light went on.

Herbert came over and gazed into the storage room. It was just as I remembered it: telephones, dust, litter and a tap. But there was something else. Somebody – a workman perhaps – had left a torch on the ground. I picked it up and turned it on. The battery was new.

'It looks like we're still in luck,' I said. 'Let's go before something horrible happens.'

'Wait a minute.' Herbert pushed past me.

'What's up?'

'I'm thirsty.'

What happened next was the second big surprise of the night. Surprise? You could have knocked me sideways – in fact Herbert did knock me over sideways in his hurry to get out.

He'd gone over to the tap. He turned it on. Nothing came out. He muttered something and hit it with the heel of his hand. The tap swivelled in the wall. There was a loud click. And a moment later a whole section of the wall swung open to reveal a jagged entrance and a stairway leading down. I stared at it. Herbert had made a dash for the door. I stared at him.

'Herbert!' I exclaimed. 'You've found it!'

'That's right!' he agreed. 'I have!' He frowned. 'What have I found?'

'The answer. That's how Johnny Powers disappeared the day I followed him. He didn't go into the tunnel. He went down there.'

Herbert looked back at the stairway. 'A secret passage . . .'

'And you opened it when you twisted the tap. You're brilliant!'

Herbert smiled and for just one moment Tim Diamond, private detective, had returned and was standing there admiring his own handiwork. 'Just leave it to me, kid,' he drawled. 'I told you I'd look after you.'

I flicked the torch on and moved forward. 'Come on then,' I said.

Tim Diamond evaporated. 'We're not going in, are we?' Herbert whimpered.

We went in. There must have been some sort of pressure switch built into the staircase because after a few steps the door swung shut behind us. I was glad in a way. Herbert would probably have turned back given half a chance. And the way I was feeling right then I'd have probably taken the other half and followed him.

Led on by the beam of the torch we went down. And down. The stairs, which had been narrow to begin with, got narrower. It was like being on the inside of a tube of toothpaste. The further down we went the more buckled and bent the walls became. I could feel them pressing in on me. I just wondered what we'd find when we got squeezed out the other end.

The air was damp now. It was sticking to my skin, trying not to go in my nose. It smelt of the river.

But there was light ahead, a strange blue glow framed by a stone archway. I flicked off the torch and turned round to warn Herbert to keep quiet. I was half a second too late. Suddenly there was a muffled explosion. It was so loud for a moment I thought the bomb in the back-pack had gone off. I felt for my shoulders. They were still attached to my arms. Then I realized. It was Herbert. He had sneezed.

'Herbert !' I hissed.

'I'b sorry,' he whispered. 'I thig I'b caught a cold.'

'Well try and keep it quiet.'

'Sure, Nig.'

We reached the bottom of the staircase and passed through the archway. If the steps had looked like they'd been carved out by some nineteenth century smuggler, the corridor that now faced us was brand new, white-tiled with neon strips burning at half-strength in the ceiling. The floor was raw concrete. I was about to move forward when a door opened at the far end. Grabbing Herbert, I ducked back behind the arch.

'What is it, Johnny?' I heard a voice ask.

'I thought I heard someone, Ma,' Johnny answered.

'What?'

'I don't know. Somebody sneezed . . .'

'It was nothing Johnny. Ya're imagining things.'

'Ya think so, Ma?'

'Sure, Johnny-boy. Come and finish ya hot chocolate and gin.'

The door closed and we breathed again. But at least I knew now that Johnny Powers and his mother were here. The door at the end of the corridor had to lead to some sort of living quarters. It was just as well we hadn't wandered in or we'd have probably ended up in quarters and certainly not living.

A second corridor led off to the right. We took it. It stretched for fifty yards, the blue neon throwing blue shadows ahead of us. The underground complex was bizarre – a bit like a hospital, a bit like the tube station it was directly under. There were no windows, of course. I could hear a faint hum in the air, some sort of ventilation system. How far did the complex reach? And how complex was it? It was impossible to say.

And impossible was the only word to describe what we found at the end of the corridor. I'd known it was large, but this was something else. In fact it was so far beyond belief that I couldn't have imagined it in my wildest dreams, and I can tell you now, some of my dreams have been pretty wild.

The white tiles had ended. Forget the hospital. Forget the tube station. What we were looking at was a crazy museum, a vast chamber with archways running down both sides and classical pillars supporting a curving brick roof. It was an Aladdin's cave, a fantastic warehouse. It had to be the central depot. The place where the Fence kept his hoards.

Paintings lined the walls, some hanging, some leaning against the brickwork. I'm no art buff but I recognized two Rembrandts and a Picasso amongst the first few I saw. Antique statues stood in a cluster. chandeliers hung from the archways. Oriental masks and mosaics poked out behind the pillars. Plain wooden crates spilled out gold and silver jewellery.

We passed a mountain of video recorders and stereo equipment. We saw enough fur coats to wipe out a generation of minks, enough cutlery to equip a chain of hotels. You could have burgled every house in London, robbed every store and stripped every museum and you still wouldn't have as much stuff as we saw there.

We'd found what we were looking for. As far as I was concerned, that was it. Now we could go to the police and give them everything they wanted . . . the Fence, Powers and the proceeds from just about every robbery in the last ten years. All we had to do was get out again. It was as simple as that.

But of course nothing in my life is simple. And when things look easy, that's just when the problems begin.

My problems began with Herbert. We'd got about half-way through the cavern when he suddenly uttered a strangled gasp and ran forward. I thought he was going to sneeze again but then he snatched something off a table and held it up to the light. When he turned round he was holding a vase, nine inches high, bright blue with some sort of bird painted on the side.

'I've found it!' he whispered, his voice on the edge of a giggle. 'I've agdually foud it!'

'Foud what?' I asked.

'The Purble Peagog.' He tried to clear his nose. 'Peagog . . .'

'Peacock?'

'You remember! The Ming . . .'

And it was. The Ming vase stolen from the British Museum had somehow found its way to the Fence and there it was, waiting to be sold. I didn't know what to say. Herbert was grinning like a kid with a new toy. For the first time in his career he had actually succeeded. But this was no time for congratulations.

'Put your hands up!' somebody said.

I spun round. Nails Nathan was standing there. In the blue light his acne looked like the surface of the moon. But it was his hand, not his face, that caught my eye. It was holding a gun. And the gun was pointing at me.

'Nails . . .' I muttered, showing him my palms. 'Maybe we can do a deal.'

'No deal, Simple,' he snarled. 'You're dead meat.'

He was right. And Herbert was the vegetable that went with it. It was all his fault. Johnny Powers had heard him sneeze. His mother hadn't been so sure, but Powers hadn't been taking any chances. He'd sent Nails out to investigate. And Herbert and his wretched Ming vase had drawn him to us.

I looked round out of the corner of my eye, hoping for a gold-plated poker or anything I could hit him with. But there was nothing. Anyway Nails had me pinned down. He'd have blasted me before I could so much as blink. All he had to do was call out for Johnny and we'd be finished.

Then Herbert sneezed for a second time. It was so unexpected and so loud that Nails jerked round before he knew what he was doing. At the same time, I was on him. With one hand I grabbed his throat. With the other I went for the gun. And that's how we stayed for a few seconds, like mad dancers doing the tango. He was trying to shout

out, but I'd got a firm grip on his wind-pipe and no wind was getting through. I spun him round. Now I was facing Herbert who was still standing there, clutching his precious Ming.

'Hit him, Herbert!' I hissed.

Nails was bigger than me and I could feel him getting away. There were only a few seconds left. The gun swayed between us as he tried to force it down towards me. I pushed with all my strength and it arced up again.

'Hit him!' I hissed again. 'Use the vase!'

Herbert moved forward. He was holding the vase in both hands and now he lifted it up, holding it above Nails's head. I waited for it to come shattering down. But Herbert didn't do it. His arms were shaking. His face was a torment as he struggled with himself.

'I can't do it!' he muttered. 'I can't do it, Nig.'

Then the gun went off.

The bullet went so close to my face that I felt the heat against my cheek. It must have missed by a fraction of an inch, firing past my head and smashing a mirror on a wall behind me. The explosion was deafening. The underground warehouse amplified even the smallest sound and the bullet and the shattering glass must have been heard in Rotherhithe. I knew than that it was hopeless. With the echo of the gun-shot still pounding in my head, I heard doors opening, footsteps running, voices calling out. Nails broke free. Once again the gun was aimed at me. I didn't move. Another dozen guns had joined it.

They had come from all directions, men that I

had never seen before unless I had glimpsed them in the darkness of the quay. They were all dressed. Perhaps they slept with their clothes on. Perhaps they never slept. But now they surrounded me. Nails rubbed his throat. There was murder in his eyes. I didn't need to ask to know whose murder he had in mind.

'I'm sorry, Nig,' Herbert whimpered. 'I couldn't . . . not the Purble Peagog.'

'Terrific, Herbert,' I muttered. 'Maybe they'll use it to put your ashes in.'

It wasn't a very nice thing to say. But I wasn't in a very nice mood. Herbert gazed into the vase and put it back on the table. The circle of men separated. Johnny Powers and his mother had appeared. They were both in dressing-gowns. Ma Powers had rollers in her hair. I almost wanted to laugh. But somehow I guessed that if I did it would be the last sound I'd ever make.

'So ya came after me!' Powers snarled. 'Ya rotten, stinking, two-timing rat.'

'You seem to have gone off me,' I muttered.

'Sure I gone off ya. I thought ya was my friend. And all the time ya was working for the cops.' Powers was quivering with anger. His face was white. But the madness was burning in his eyes. 'I hate cops,' he went on. 'If I had my way I'd kill ya now – both of ya. And I'd do it slow.'

'Why don't ya?' Ma Powers demanded. She was some mother.

'Because the Fence will want to see him.' Powers glanced at Nails. 'You OK?' he asked.

'Sure, Johnny.' Nails sounded far from OK. His

voice seemed to have got trapped in the lower reaches of his throat. He coughed. 'I found 'em with the vase.'

'The vase?' Powers shook his head, dismissing it. 'I want them tied up and locked up. The Fence will be here tomorrow. We'll finish them then.'

Nails signalled and four men moved in on us. We didn't even try to struggle. We were frog-marched to the far end of the gallery. It ended with a narrow corridor that led past a bank of machinery, the ventilation unit and the electrical controls. On the other side I caught sight of an iron grill with an empty space behind it, the sort of thing you might see in an underground car-park. We arrived at a door. Nails opened it and we were pushed into a small room.

One of the men had produced some rope. I'd always thought Nails was highly strung but that was nothing compared to what we were five minutes later. Our ankles, our knees, our wrists, our arms . . . Nails didn't miss a muscle. We ended up sitting with our backs to the wall. And that was the way it looked like we were going to stay.

The men left and Powers came in. He looked at us with a thin smile of satisfaction. His eyes were still ugly.

'Johnny . . .' I began. I was going to remind him of our time together in Strangeday Hall, how we'd been good friends, how I'd saved his life. But it wouldn't have cut any ice with him. This guy had ice for blood.

'Save ya breath, Simple,' he cut in. 'Ya're gonna need it when the Fence gets here.'

'Who is the Fence?' I asked. It wasn't going to do me any good now but I still wanted to know.

'Ya'll find out soon enough.' Powers grinned unpleasantly.

'It's quite an outfit you got here,' I said.

Powers nodded. 'Right now ya're sitting a hundred feet under the Thames. It's right above you.'

'The Fence built this place?'

'No. Some guy called Brunel did a hundred years ago. Nobody knew about it except the Fence. There were two tunnels, ya see. This was the first one. Only it ran into problems. Something about the limestone. So he started again a bit higher up. The Fence found the old tunnel, had it adapted.' He stopped and sneered at me. 'But why am I wasting my breath telling ya all this? Ya'll hear it from the Fence tomorrow.'

He leant down and gripped my face with an iron hand. I could feel his fingers gouging into my cheeks.

'The Fence will deal with you real good,' he whispered. Then he laughed, a high-pitched, trembling laugh. 'But maybe there'll be something left for me. I'm gonna make ya wish ya'd never heard of me, Simple. After I've finished with ya, ya'll wish ya'd never been born.'

'Like you?' I said. 'You weren't born, Powers. You hatched.'

I should have saved the wise-cracks. His fist cracked into the side of my head. 'I'll tear you apart piece by piece,' he promised. 'Nobody crosses Johnny Powers and gets away with it.'

He turned on his heels and strode out of the room. The door banged shut and I heard a key being turned and two bolts being drawn across. Then there was silence.

My head was ringing and I could already feel the bruise where he'd hit me. But I'd had to get him angry. I'd had to keep his attention. Because there was one thing he hadn't noticed.

My back-pack had been torn off my shoulders and flung into one corner of the room. Nobody had thought to examine it. It was still there.

And the bomb was still inside it.

17
Under Water

The last time I'd been tied up in a room, it had been with an escapologist's assistant called Lauren Bacardi. We'd spent a bit of time together and she'd shown me one or two tricks of the trade. I'm not saying I was any Houdini. But I had learnt something. For example, when Nails and the others were tying me up this time round, I'd remembered to keep all my muscles flexed. Now that they'd gone, I relaxed them. It didn't do much good. But it gave me a little play.

There was also something else. I was more or less dry after my dip in the Thames, but it had left me with a sheen of oil or grease. Like I said, the water was dirty. Now I was grateful for it. My skin was still covered with a slippery coating that made it easier to slide underneath the ropes. Easier but not that easy. It was going to take time.

Herbert hadn't said anything for a while. That suited me. I still blamed him for getting us into this mess, him and his sneezing and his precious vase. But looking at him, I couldn't help feeling sorry for him. He looked about as happy as a turkey on Christmas Eve.

'Don't worry, Herbert,' I said. 'We'll soon be out of here.' I tugged and felt one of the cords slide over my wrist. Now all I had to do was get it over my hand without dislocating my thumb.

'How?' Herbert sighed. He had been watching me struggle. 'Eben if we weren't died up, there's still the door. Logged add boated. And thed there's a whole arby of grooks waiting for us on the other side. All arbed. It's useless. It's hobeless. It's the end.'

'That's what I like to hear,' I said. 'Always the optimist . . .'

Even so, I had to admit that it looked as if he was right. Fifteen minutes of fighting with the ropes and the only thing that was doing any running in that room was Herbert's nose.

But I struggled on. There was nothing else to do. Herbert dozed off, huddled up against the wall. Time passed. I didn't know how much time. There was no clock, no window, just a single bulb burning through the night. Maybe it was an hour. Maybe it was more. But just as I was about to give up, my left hand came free. The skin was torn and I had more bruises than a peach in an all-night corner-shop. But my fingers moved. I was on my way out.

After that things went more quickly. I freed my legs next and finally my right arm. When I stood up, I felt like I'd just come out of the spin drier. But I'd done it. I'd actually done it. That just left the locked and bolted door and the army of crooks.

For the first time I looked around the room. It was long and narrow, about the same size as my cell at Strangeday Hall. There was a second door at the far end which I'd taken for a cupboard. But opening it now, I found it led into a small corridor running a few yards at right angles to the room itself. It must have been a storage area or something. It stopped with another solid wall. There was no way out from there. But it gave me an idea. I knew what I had to do.

I woke Herbert up and began to untie him. As I worked, I told him what I had in mind.

'Are you oud ob your mide?' he asked. His cold had got much worse. 'Forged id! Just die be up agaid. I'll waid for the Fedze.'

'No way, Herbert,' I replied. I wasn't quite sure what he said, but I hadn't liked the sound of it. 'Whoever the Fence is, he's one person I don't want to meet.' I remembered what Powers had told me. He hadn't given anything away. 'Or she,' I added.

'Budnig . . .'

'Budnig?'

'Bud Nig . . . !'

'No arguments, Herbert. Once the door's open we'll have to move fast. And we've got to go back up there.' I jerked my thumb towards the ceiling.

'You're bad,' Herbert said.

'Bad? What have I done that's bad?' I demanded.

'Not bad. Bad! Starg staring bad.'

Herbert was free by now. I helped him to his feet and left him rubbing his wrists, his ankles and his nose. Somehow he was managing to do all three at the same time. I went over to the back-pack and opened it. Herbert stopped what he was doing when he saw the bomb. I don't know what astonished him more. My idea or the fact that I'd been carrying it around with me all day.

Mickey Mouse's hand was touching the figure eleven. I eased it back a bit, then reached for the switch. That took a bit of doing, I can tell you. I couldn't be sure the bomb wouldn't go off the moment it was turned back on. But the only explosion was another sneeze from Herbert. He really knew how to time them. I carried the bomb over to the door and left it there.

'You're bad,' Herbert said again.

'It's the only way out,' I insisted. 'The blast will tear out the door. But the walls look solid enough. There shouldn't be too much damage.'

'Whad about us?'

'We go in there.'

There, was the corridor. I took one last look at the bomb, hoping I wasn't making a terrible mistake. Johnny Powers had said we were underneath the Thames. If the ceiling collapsed, it would be interesting to see if we were crushed before or after we were drowned. Either was preferable to being shot or strangled when the Fence arrived. And anyway I was sure I was doing the right thing. The force of the blast would be carried outwards. It would smash the door and perhaps shatter a few mirrors. Herbert and I would escape in the confusion. The more I thought about it, the more I liked it. Only I was careful not to think about it too much.

We went to the end of the corridor and crouched beside the wall, waiting. That was the worst part. I thought I'd given us two minutes' grace. It felt like two hours.

'Herbert . . .' I began. I wanted to tell him what a great brother he'd been, how I'd always admired him. It wasn't true. I just thought he'd like to hear it. But he couldn't hear anything. His fingers were jammed into his ears so tight that I figured they'd meet in the middle. His eyes were shut. 'All right,' I muttered. 'Have it . . .'

The bomb went off.

The noise was deafening. It wasn't just loud. It almost tore my ears off. A cloud of dust stampeded down the corridor, throwing me off my feet. It seemed to go on for ever. The lights flickered, went out, then glowed faintly. As the echo faded out I was aware of the clatter of falling masonry and – the last sound I wanted to hear – the splash of water. With the dust streaking my eyes and clogging up the back of my throat, I got back to my feet. I looked round for Herbert. Somehow the explosion had managed to tear his shirt in half. Or maybe he'd done it himself. It hung on him like two ragged curtains. His hair was all over the place. And by that I didn't just mean his head.

'Let's go!' I yelled, although it came out as a muffled croak.

There was no need for silence now. Already I could hear people shouting in the distance. Nearer to us, the ventilation equipment seemed to have gone into overdrive, the cogs and fan-wheels screaming and grinding. The lights flickered again. We staggered back down the corridor and into the cell – or what was left of it. The bomb hadn't just taken out the door. It had demolished the entire wall. I looked up. There was a nasty crack in the ceiling, zig-zagging across. Water was seeping through, a thin sheet that splattered on to the broken concrete floor. But even as I watched the downpour became wider, faster. A brick fell, narrowly missing Herbert. Clutching him, I edged forward.

Outside the cell, everything was as chaotic as I'd hoped. It was hard to tell where the dust ended and the smoke began. But the effect was the same. Stretch out your arm and you couldn't see your hand. Some of the machines had caught fire. Through the swirling smoke I saw a sudden eruption of brilliant sparks. The ventilation system shuddered, snapped and fell silent. More sparks of electric white burst out, buzzing like miniature fireworks. There was a rush of crimson flame. Behind us, the water poured down faster than ever. As we stood there hesitating it lapped our heels. Water behind, fire ahead, smoke everywhere. Mickey Mouse had gone out like a lion.

I knew where I wanted to head, while I still had a head to get there. Through the gate that looked like the entrance to a car-park. It was directly ahead of us, but before I could stop him, Herbert broke free and ran off to the right. The smoke swallowed him up.

'Herbert!' I yelled.

'The Purple Peacock!' he shouted back. 'I can't leave it!'

I couldn't believe what I was hearing. I'd got us out. We could still make it to the surface. All Hell was breaking loose. And he was going after the wretched Ming vase! For a moment I was tempted to leave him to it. But I couldn't. He was my brother. I was responsible for him. But if someone else didn't kill him first, I'd do it once we were out of this mess. I plunged into the smoke after him. At least the explosion seemed to have cured his cold.

The smoke was like a curtain. After a few steps it

suddenly parted and I found myself back in the main gallery. Things weren't so bad on the other side. The bomb had managed to smash perhaps a million pounds worth of priceless china and glass. Tentacles of water were already creeping past to claim the Persian rugs and carpets. But the place was still standing. And the lights were still on.

I just had time to see Herbert disappear behind the column when someone appeared, holding a machine gun. It was Nails Nathan. He swung round and I dived to one side, crashing headlong into a harp that collapsed with a great zing. It was accompanied by a crackle of bullets that swept past about six inches above my head. A Rembrandt self-portrait on the wall behind me looked down sadly with about eighteen extra eyes. Nails ran forward. Keeping my head down, I scrambled on, desperately searching for a weapon or for somewhere to hide – ideally both.

'Find him! Kill him! Kill both of them!'

It was Johnny Powers. He had appeared on the scene – and he wasn't happy. His voice was hysterical, like a kid who's lost his parents. The ventilation system wasn't the only thing that had cracked that night. I knew complete insanity when I heard it. And I was hearing it now.

Nails Nathan was almost on top of me when I found it. It must have been stolen from some fancy antique shop. A medieval crossbow complete with bolt. It wasn't quite the weapon I'd had in mind, but it would do. It had a sort of ratchet with a lever to arm it. I pulled it back, then loaded the bolt. Nails was moving more cautiously now. I crouched down behind a marble table, waiting to get him in my sights. The suddenly there he was, looking up in front of me. He brought the machine gun round. I squeezed the trigger. The crossbow jerked. So did Nails. The bolt hit him in the chest. He keeled over backwards. At the same time, he fired the machine gun. But now it was pointing upwards. A chandelier tore itself apart, the crystals ricocheting off the walls. Nails slumped and lay still. I lowered the cross-bow. It looked like his acne wouldn't be troubling him any more.

But this was no time for self-congratulations. Johnny Powers was getting closer and now his mother was with him.

'You look out for yaself, Johnny-boy,' I heard her say.

'Don't ya worry, ma,' he replied. 'I'm gonna find that lousy, dirty, double-crossing . . .' His words became incoherent.

Ducking down behind the columns, I ran through the gallery. I could see Johnny Powers now. He'd got dressed and he was holding a pistol. There were six men with him, fanning out to search the place. The others had run on to deal with the flames. Ma Powers hung back in her dressing-gown and curlers.

Fortunately I found Herbert before they did. He was standing with the Purple Peacock, gazing at it like he was in some posh department store and he was thinking of buying it. It was incredible. Didn't he realize that we were still trapped underground with an awful lot of very awful people out to kill us? There are times when I think that in his own way

Herbert is as mad as Johnny Powers. This was one of them.

'Herbert!' I whispered. 'Have you quite finished?'

'Sure, Nick.' He clutched the vase to him. He was actually smiling. It meant that much to him, finding it.

'Then do you mind if we go?'

'Ya're not going anywhere!'

Powers was standing only a few feet away. He hadn't seen me, but he had seen Herbert. And now he'd got both of us. The six armed men formed a semi-circle around us. They were all holding guns. They looked like an execution squad. In fact, they were an execution squad.

'Ya're finished, Simple,' Powers snarled. His face was distorted with hatred. 'I should've plugged ya when I had ya before. But this time I'm not making any more mistakes. I'm gonna do it now.' He giggled. 'And I'm gonna enjoy it.'

He raised his gun.

I knew it was the end. But I still didn't expect it to happen so quickly. And it wasn't the end I'd expected.

First there was a gun-shot. But it wasn't Johnny's gun. It came from the end of the corridor. The gun was torn out of Johnny's hand, clattering on the floor. The six men wheeled round. My eyes followed them.

Chief Inspector Snape of Scotland Yard stood there. He was alive. He was armed. There were about twenty uniformed policemen with him.

'All right, Powers,' he said. 'Come on out with

your hands up. I've got this place surrounded. You haven't got a chance.'

Then the roof collapsed.

I suppose it had only been a matter of time. Powers had spoken of a problem in the building of the tunnel – the tunnel that was now the Fence's headquarters. Something to do with the limestone. Whatever it was, it had been a splinter that had just been waiting for an excuse to turn into a yawning chasm – and the explosion had been that excuse. The whole complex shook. Then about a ton of bricks and broken stone crashed down on Powers, burying him. I didn't see what happened to the six men. Because a second later the Thames followed. All of it.

If I hadn't been standing to one side. I'd have been killed there and then. Even so I was hurled off my feet. The last thing I saw was Herbert, clasping the Purple Peacock. Then I was swept away, carried helplessly in a torrent of racing, foaming water. Somebody screamed. Another section of the ceiling smashed down. A column tottered and collapsed, ploughing into a grand piano and reducing it instantly to matchwood. Televisions and video recorders surged past, spinning in the current. Everything was spinning. The water was roaring in my ears. I'm going to drown, I thought. This is it. Prepare to meet your maker. And don't forget to ask him why you got such a raw deal.

But then a hand grabbed me and pulled me up into the air. It was Snape. He had formed a human chain with the other policemen. It reached back to the metal grill which was also the way they'd come in. After the initial impact, the flow of the water eased off. It was about six feet deep. The Titanic must have looked a bit like this with furs and jewellery floating in the icy water. And bodies. Johnny Powers drifted past. He was floating face-down.

Another column snapped in half, unable to stand the pressure. More stonework cascaded down.

'Herbert!' I shouted.

For there he was, swimming towards me with one hand. It was incredible. He wasn't only alive. He still had the Purple Peacock. And despite everything – the explosions, the falling masonry, the flood – it was still in one piece.

'This way, laddy,' Snape said.

I grabbed Herbert and together we were pulled through the water towards the metal grill. Even now the danger wasn't over. In another few seconds the whole gallery would go under. One of the walls was bulging. The water was building up for a second wave. The fires had gone out but the smoke was still curling across the littered surface.

I was too exhausted to do anything for myself any more. I allowed Snape to pull me through the water. I still couldn't believe he was alive. And how had he found me? But explanations could wait until later. Two more policemen took hold of me and a moment later I found myself sitting on dry land. Then Herbert was pulled out to join me, still holding the Purple Peacock.

We were on a sort of wooden platform. It must have been seven feet above the ground because it was a foot above the water. It was behind the metal grill which Snape now closed. All twenty policemen were there, along with Herbert, Snape and myself – and you could still have found room for more. There were two buttons set in a box on the wall. One was red, the other green.

'This had better work,' Snape muttered.

He pushed the green button.

I heard another roar as the second deluge began. The water leapt up at us. But at the same time the whole platform moved, sliding upwards into blackness. For thirty seconds I couldn't see anything but I could feel my stomach sink. And now I knew. Of course. It had reminded me of an underground car park. Because the platform was nothing less than a huge lift.

At last it broke into the light of the early morning. I looked around, blinking. And then I wanted to laugh. We had travelled up a shaft, up through the water. And I knew where we were. I should have known all along.

We were inside the *Penelope*.

'All right, Snape.' I said. 'Spit it out. How come you're alive? How did you get here. What's been going on?'

I was sitting on a bench near the river, wrapped in a blanket and holding a tin mug of hot tea. The Purple Peacock was in a cardboard box beside me. It was eight o'clock in the morning and for once Wapping was a hive of activity. There were police cars everywhere. A mobile canteen had been set up, supplying tea and bacon sandwiches. There were also two ambulances. I was fine, but Herbert was being treated for shock.

The banks of the Thames were lined by constables holding nets. They were more like fishermen than policemen. For the past hour all sorts of treasures had been floating to the surface, only to be caught and taken away for identification. And they weren't the only things to fall into the police net. So far seven of the Fence's gang had made it out, using the staircase that led into the tube station. Ma Powers had been the last to emerge, her face blank, her eyes glassy. By the time she got out of prison she would be Great Grandmother Powers. Strangely enough, I almost felt sorry for her. She'd only been looking after her boy. Which was more than my mother had ever done for me.

Only the Fence had escaped. That was the worst of it. He hadn't been in the underground complex at the time and it was unlikely now that he would show up. The whole area had been cordoned off. Crowds of journalists and television cameras were being held back behind the barriers. The river police were patrolling the Thames and helicopters buzzed overhead. The whole of London knew what had happened, was being told about it on breakfast TV. By now, the Fence was probably on his way to Rio.

'Where do I start?' Snape asked.

'How about with the way you framed me?' I growled. He might have saved my life a few minutes ago. But that didn't even the score. If it hadn't been for him I'd have still been happily at school – or at least, as happy as you can be when you're in a dump like mine.

Snape wasn't even a little bit apologetic. 'I had to frame you,' he said. 'You wouldn't play along otherwise.'

'But that's criminal!'

'No. That's police-work. But don't worry, my old son. All the charges against you will be dropped now. And I did my best to look out for you. I was never far behind.'

'Yeah. How come you showed up like that?' I sipped the tea. It was warm and sweet. I wouldn't have used either word to describe Snape.

'You were bugged,' Snape explained. 'I had you on radar every minute of the day.'

'Bugged? How?'

'In your shoes.' Snape pointed. 'Your prison shoes. There's a powerful tracking device in each of the heels.'

'So . . .' Suddenly it came to me. 'That night on the railway tracks in Clapham. It was you who cut me free!'

Snape nodded. 'That's right. I saw you snatched by Big Ed's gang. We followed you there. Once they'd left you on the tracks, I came looking for you. I helped you get out.'

'Well thanks for that . . .'

'It was the same thing tonight,' Snape went on. 'We homed in on you under the river and I guessed you'd found the Fence. After that we came in to get you.'

'You took your time.'

'We were waiting for the Fence.'

'Yeah – well, it looks like the one who got away.'

'Don't worry about him, laddy. We've smashed

his operation. And one of the gang will talk. You'll see. We'll catch up with him eventually.'

'Just so long as you don't need any more help from me.' I finished the tea. It was the first hot drink I'd had in thirty-six hours. 'So how come you weren't killed?' I asked. 'I saw you . . . in the car.'

Snape paused, suddenly serious for a moment. 'That was a close call,' he admitted. 'We never expected Powers to break out of Strangeday Hall. When we heard what was happening – and that you were with him – we came along to see what we could do. Then, when we hit that telephone box . . .'

He took a deep breath.

'I was lucky. I was in the back seat. The door was ripped off and I was thrown clear just before the car blew. The driver managed to get out too. Then we went back and got Boyle.'

'He's dead?'

'No. He's in hospital. Third degree burns.'

'You're breaking my heart, Snape,' I said. 'I'll send him some flowers.'

'That's good of you, lad.'

'Sure. Dandelions.'

Perhaps I was being a bit hard. But think about it. I'd been framed, tried and sent to jail, menaced, chased, shot at, kidnapped, knocked out, tied to a railway track, almost blown up, menaced some more, tied up again, half-drowned, exhausted – and all for two policemen who hadn't even caught their man anyway. It wasn't as if I'd been given any choice. And what was I going to get out of it all, except for extra homework once I got back to school?

'You won't do so badly,' Snape assured me. 'There'll be a reward from the insurance companies for some of the stuff that gets recovered. And the police will recompense you.'

'I've had enough of the British police, thanks all the same,' I said. 'If they're meant to be the best in the world, I'd hate to see how the KGB operates.'

We sat in silence, watching the activity all around us. I yawned. I was dog tired. All I wanted was a bed. I'd even settle for a kennel.

Then Herbert strolled over to us.

He'd been fixed up by the doctors. Someone had lent him a jersey. And he was looking in a lot better shape than me. In fact he was quite his old self. Which is to say that as usual he was totally impossible.

'Hi, Nick!' he said, smiling.

'Are you OK, Herbert?' I asked.

'Tim,' he corrected me. 'This has been Tim Diamond's greatest case. It'll make me famous. The man who got Johnny Powers!'

'What about me?' I demanded.

'You helped, kid. Maybe I'll even share some of the reward with you. In fact I'll forget that fiver you owe me.' He tapped me gently on the shoulder. I felt like knocking him out. 'The British Museum will pay me plenty for the return of the Purple Peacock,' he went on. 'By the way, where is it?'

He sat down as he spoke. But he was so wrapped up in himself that he wasn't looking what he was doing. I saw his backside come down fair and square on the cardboard box. The cardboard crumpled.

There was a dull splintering from inside. The colour drained out of Herbert's face.

The Purple Peacock had been stolen in Camden. It had found its way to Wapping. It had survived an explosion and a flood. But it hadn't survived Herbert.

He'd just sat on it.

18
French Translation

It ended exactly the way it had begun – with French on a hot afternoon.

C'ÉTAIT UN DIMANCHE MATIN ET IL FAISAIT CHAUD. ANTOINE ET PHILLIPE ÉTAIENT DANS LE CHAMP. LEUR PÈRE DORMAIT DANS UNE CHAISE-LONGUE. QUELQU'UN LES APPELLA DE L'AUTRE CÔTÉ DE LA PALISSADE. C'ÉTAIT LEUR GRAND-MÈRE.
'VOULEZ-VOUS JOUER AU FOOTBALL?' DEMANDA-T-ELLE.

The exercise was written up on the blackboard and we were being made to translate it out loud. Palis would call out a name and some poor soul would have to stand up and stumble over the next sentence. You weren't allowed to sit down until you reached a full stop. Why do French translations have to be so stupid? You sweat your guts out turning them into English only to find they weren't worth it in the first place. Fortunately I'd done this one the night before. If my name was called, I could cope.

'*Sington!*'

'*It was a . . . er . . . Dimanche . . . Sunday morning and it made warm.*'

'*It was hot, you stupid child!*'

A fortnight had passed since our escape from

Penelope. In the newspapers, the story had slipped from page one headlines to page two comment to a few column inches on page three. Anyway, the press had left out more than it had told. For a start, nobody mentioned Herbert or me. Snape had seen to that with something called a D-notice. D for don't! He said it would be better for me if my name was kept out of things. And better for you too, I thought. What would the British public make of the British police framing and blackmailing British school-kids? I mean, it simply wasn't British.

'*Sit down, Sington. Goodman!*'

'*Me, sir?*'

'*Yes you, Goodman.*'

'*Antoine and Phillipe were in the field, sir.*'

In the end I'd got a four-line mention in some of the nationals. They said that I'd been released from Strangeday Hall 'in the light of new evidence'. In other words, my name was cleared. Only Snape and the authorities were making sure that it wasn't a name you'd read about too much.

'*Hopkins!*'

'*Their father was asleep in a garden chair.*'

'*Exactement.*'

Of course, I'd been the centre of attention once I'd got back to school. The headmaster had made a speech about me during assembly. Everyone had made a lot of jokes. But it's surprising how quickly people forget these things. After a few days everything was back to normal. Sure enough, there was extra homework. Enough to fill an extra home. But I wasn't the hero any more. I wasn't sure that I ever had been.

Palis hadn't changed either. He was his old, sarcastic, ear-tweaking self. He had barely said a word to me since I'd got back. It was as if he wanted to forget the evening we had spent together. I hadn't mentioned his involvement, the way he had helped me. I guessed he preferred it that way. But he could at least have said he was glad to see me alive.

'Simple!'

He called my name now and I got to my feet. It was hot and stuffy in the classroom. The sun was dazzling me. It was hard to concentrate on the French words. Somebody did something from the other side of the palissade? I remembered.

'Someone called them from the other side of the fence,' I said.

'Yes. That is correct, Simple. Now – Buckingham! The next sentence . . .'

I sat down again.

My head was throbbing and I could feel the sweat beading on my skin. For a moment I thought I was ill. But it was something else. The voices in the classroom had become a dull echo. I screwed up my eyes and tried to focus on the blackboard. I'd seen something, read something that was horribly wrong. Or maybe just horrible.

The French words in Palis's spidery handwriting blurred, then straightened out. I plucked out the sentence I had just translated.

'QUELQU'UN LES APPELLA DE L'AUTRE CÔTÉ DE LA PALISSADE.'

The fence! That was it. I'd just said the word myself.

The fence – *la palissade*.

Palissade.

Palis.

No. It was insane – a coincidence. I glanced at the French teacher. He was talking to someone else but his eyes were fixed on me. And there was a cruel smile tugging at his lips.

And then suddenly it all made sense. Palis was the Fence. It couldn't have been anyone else.

When Snape had first come to visit me he had told me that the Fence could be hiding behind an ordinary occupation – a banker or a shopkeeper for example. He could also have been a teacher. In fact with their afternoons off and long holidays, what better cover could there have been? And Snape had probably suspected him from the start. The thought hit me like a bucket of ice. Why else would he have chosen me of all people to do his dirty work? He'd guessed that Powers would break out of Strangeday Hall. He'd hoped that I'd go with him. That was why he'd been there so coincidentally the night of the escape. I would recognize the Fence when I saw him. And if the recognition killed me, it would only prove that Snape had been right all along.

Palis . . .

Piece by piece it all fitted together. Right at the start, in Woburn Abbey, I had been surprised how much the French teacher had known about art and antiques. But of course, as the Fence, that had been his profession. I'd seen art books in his flat too. I'd obviously caught him doing his own homework.

And I'd cooked my goose the moment I'd walked in there. For once I'd been unfair to Herbert. He hadn't blown it with Johnny Powers. I had. I'd told

Palis everything, blurting it all out before he had time to reveal himself to me. Because that was what he was going to do. When he'd saved me from the police, he'd said there was a reason – and the reason was because he'd thought I was on his side. If I'd only kept my mouth shut, he would have told me everything. But like a fool, I'd delivered myself to him on a plate.

No wonder he'd been in a hurry to leave Wapping the next morning. He'd known about the bomb because he'd telephoned Powers the night before. I'd even heard the tinkle of the bell in my dreams. Poor old Herbert had been dragged out of his bed on my account. Palis had cold-bloodedly arranged it all. He'd driven me there knowing that it was the last journey I'd ever make . . . at least, in one piece.

But still I could have guessed. In the underground gallery, Powers had accused me of working for the police. Even if he had seen through Herbert's disguise there was no way he could have known that. Herbert certainly hadn't told him. Nor had I. That only left one person, the only other person who knew.

Palis . . .

The thud of closing books and the slamming of desks brought me back to the present. I glanced at the clock. It was three thirty, the end of the last lesson. Already people were running down the corridors as the school emptied. What was Palis planning? Did he know that I knew? I looked at him carefully. There could be no doubt about it. He had handed me that sentence as a challenge. He was finished and he knew it. But he planned to take me with him.

'That is all for today,' he was saying now. 'Malheureusement I will not be with you next week. In fact I am taking a holiday . . . a long holiday. I will not be coming back.'

There was a groan of disappointment from the class – fake, of course. Nobody would be really disappointed if he fell off a cliff.

'You can go now,' he went on. 'All except Simple.' He dropped the three words like daggers.

My fingers tightened on the desk. Everyone else had got up and begun to shuffle forward. Palis slid his hand into his jacket. It was a casual movement but I had no doubt what he was holding on the inside. What could I do? If I tried to make a break for the door now, he would start shooting – and he wouldn't be too fussy about who he hit. But once I was alone, I wouldn't have any chance at all. By the next day I'd be back in the newspapers again. In the obituaries.

There was just one chance. He had more or less told me that he was the Fence. He knew that I knew. But did he know that I knew that he knew that I knew? Work it out. It made sense to me.

I walked forward innocently and stood in front of his desk. A pile of exercise books were stacked between us. I rested my hands in front of them. There were only seven or eight people left in the classroom, grouped around the door.

'Is it about the French translation, sir?' I asked.

'No, Simple.' He blinked at me, wondering if I

was more stupid than he thought. That was what I wanted him to think.

'I did do all the extra work you set me, sir,' I went on.

'It's not about that, Simple.'

I pretended to scratch my nose, using the cover to look out of the corner of my eye. The doorway was clear.

'Mr Palis . . . ?' I said.

At the same moment, I jerked both my hands upwards. He was already pulling out the gun but I'd taken him by surprise. The books flew into his face, knocking him off balance. At the same time I ran for it. I'd reached the door before he'd recovered. Even so, there was a sudden crack and the frame splintered as I passed through.

I was out. But I wasn't away. Palis had a gun equipped with a silencer. Nobody had heard the first shot. Nobody knew anything was wrong. I looked left and right. The main entrance was blocked by a crowd of people, milling out into the yard. I went the other way, skidding along the corridor and crashing into a fire extinguisher. The second shot hit the extinguisher with a loud clang. I spun round a corner, colliding with Mr Snelgrove as he came out of one of the classes.

'Simple . . . !' he began.

Palis fired again. The bullet drilled through six volumes of the Oxford Medieval History and buried itself in Snelgrove's shoulder. He screamed and passed out. I jumped over him and ran.

I came to a staircase and took them, three steps

at a time. I'd reached the first floor when a photograph of an old school cricket team seemed to blow itself off the wall just above my shoulder. With a fresh burst of speed I carried on to the second floor and then to the third. Even as I went I was asking myself one question. Where was Snape? If he suspected Palis, he had to be somewhere near. It almost seemed as if the Chief Inspector wanted me dead as much as the Fence.

The top floor of the school was given over to the biology and physics laboratories. They must have finished earlier because they were empty now. There was no way out from here and no witnesses. Palis knew that. He was moving more slowly, his feet heavy on the stairs. I tiptoed through a pair of swing doors and into the biology lab, hoping he would miss me. A dissected rat stared at me from a glass case. A skull grinned beside a bunsen burner. Palis found me. There was another muffled cough and the skull disintegrated as his bullet hit it right between the eye-sockets. I threw myself behind a counter. The Fence walked into the room.

Fortunately the blinds had been drawn in the room and there wasn't much light. I crouched behind the counter, moving forward on my haunches. The counter stretched almost the whole length of the room. As I went one way, Palis walked the other. I could hear his footsteps but I couldn't see him. I didn't dare look.

There were shelves under the counter, close to the floor. Each one was lined with bottles, filled with liquid of different colours. I took one and pulled out the stopper. The smell made my eyes water. Palis stopped. He was breathing deeply. I reckoned he was only a few feet away, standing on the other side of the counter. I straightened up. And there he was, right in front of me. He fired. I threw the bottle.

His bullet hit me in the arm, spinning me into the wall. My bottle hit him in the face, splashing its contents all over him. He screamed and rammed his hands into his eyes. A wisp of smoke curled out from underneath them. Pressing my own wound with one hand, I staggered out of the laboratory.

Another door stood open opposite the laboratory. Still clutching my arm, I ran through it and up another flight of stairs. I didn't know where I was going any more. I just wanted to put as much distance between myself and Palis as I could. God knows what I'd done to his eyes. What had been inside the bottle? Sulphuric acid? Nasty . . .

The stairway led on to the roof. That was as far as I could go. It was a flat area no bigger than a tennis court with a fifty foot drop on each side. But at least there was one good thing. I could hear the police sirens. I looked down and saw the first cars come racing up to the school. There were still a lot of people around and now they were joined by a squadron of armed policemen diving out of the cars and taking up their positions around the building. As usual Snape was late. But at least he had arrived.

'Simple . . .'

Palis was standing in the doorway, trying to hold the gun steady. He was a mess. White burn-marks streaked one side of his face. One eye was closed.

The other was blood-shot and staring. Half his hair seemed to have dissolved.

'You destroyed everything,' Palis hissed. 'My whole operation . . . my life's work.'

'And now you're finished, Fence,' I said. 'This is your last post.'

'Oui. But I'll take you with me, Simple. At least I'll have the satisfaction of that.'

He squeezed the trigger.

But nothing happened. He had fired six bullets. He didn't have a seventh.

Palis screamed out and charged. He came at me like a wild bull. I stepped aside. Unable to stop himself, he shot over the edge of the building. Still screaming, he plummeted down. Then the screams stopped. I walked back to the edge and looked down. It wasn't a pretty sight. Palis had come to a horrible end. But an appropriate one all the same.

The Fence had impaled himself on a fence.

Ten minutes later I walked out of the school, my right arm hanging limp, blood spreading through my shirt. They'd wanted to carry me on a stretcher but I'd refused. I wanted to be on my own two feet.

From Woburn Abbey to Strangeday Hall to this . . . it hadn't been a lot of laughs. But I was still alive. I was more or less in one piece. And that was all that mattered. Because life isn't so bad if you don't let it get you down, and although I'd got plenty to complain about I meant to go on and milk it for all it was worth.